HAMMER IT HOME

JAYNE RYLON

Sign Up For The Naughty News!
Contests, sneak peeks, appearance info, and more.
www.jaynerylon.com/newsletter

Shop
Autographed books, reading-themed apparel,
notebooks, totes, and more.
www.jaynerylon.com/shop

Contact Jayne
Email: contact@jaynerylon.com
Website: www.jaynerylon.com
Facebook: Facebook.com/JayneRylon
Twitter: @JayneRylon

OTHER BOOKS BY JAYNE RYLON

DIVEMASTERS
Going Down
Going Deep
Going Hard

MEN IN BLUE
Night is Darkest
Razor's Edge
Mistress's Master
Spread Your Wings
Wounded Hearts
Bound For You

POWERTOOLS
Kate's Crew
Morgan's Surprise
Kayla's Gift
Devon's Pair
Nailed to the Wall
Hammer it Home

HOTRODS
King Cobra
Mustang Sally
Super Nova
Rebel on the Run
Swinger Style
Barracuda's Heart
Touch of Amber
Long Time Coming

COMPASS BROTHERS
Northern Exposure
Southern Comfort
Eastern Ambitions
Western Ties

COMPASS GIRLS
Winter's Thaw
Hope Springs
Summer Fling
Falling Softly

PLAY DOCTOR
Dream Machine
Healing Touch

STANDALONES
4-Ever Theirs
Nice & Naughty
Where There's Smoke
Report For Booty

RACING FOR LOVE
Driven
Shifting Gears

RED LIGHT
Through My Window
Star
Can't Buy Love
Free For All

PARANORMALS
Picture Perfect
Reborn
PICK YOUR PLEASURES
Pick Your Pleasure
Pick Your Pleasure 2

DEDICATION

For all my readers.

You have made this a landmark year in my writing career. By helping me reach several major milestones—like hitting the *New York Times* Bestseller list with my great friend and co-author, Mari Carr, and winning an RT Reviewer's Choice Award for Best Erotic Romance of 2011—you've propelled me several giant steps closer to my dream of one day being able to proudly declare that I am full-time writer.

Thank you for your support.

"Awwww." Morgan's three best friends melted as Kate withdrew her latest purchases from the pink-and-blue-striped, lamb-dotted Cutie Patootie shopping bag to display for their approval. They passed around the itty bittiest pajama set Morgan had ever seen.

"I love the matching fuzzy socks." Kayla grinned.

"So soft." Devon sighed as she ran the tip of her index finger across the plush fabric.

"Do you think they'll be warm enough?" Kate nibbled at the inside of her cheek, highlighting her dimples. "Or maybe too thick?"

"Don't worry so much, Katiebug," Neil chimed in from where he—along with the other four guys in the crew—slathered cheery green paint on one wall of the nursery. "Your girl's probably going to kick them off anyway. My sister's kids always seemed to strip and have their toes in their mouth in half a second flat."

"Look, it could be a boy. There's no telling yet." Mike paused with his roller in the middle of the patch of color he'd focused on. His lack of typical gusto made it seem as if even he didn't believe the mantra he'd recited for nearly three months now.

"How much longer do we have to wait to say, 'I told you so'?" Dave dodged a half-hearted swipe from Mike. Not fast enough to avoid minty splatters on his already Pollock-esque coveralls. "The ultrasound is next week, right?"

"Whoa. Stop that right there." Kate wagged her finger at the guys. "No paint fights today. The baby will not be happy if you mess up her gorgeous new hardwood floors. A little drop cloth is no match for you when you get riled up."

"Last time I checked, you liked it when I got riled up." Mike smirked until her admonishment sank in. "Hold up. *Her* floor? No. No. No. Whose side are you on?"

He pouted, the roller forgotten in his hand, which dangled by his knee as his shoulders slumped.

"The one that gives us a healthy baby of either gender." She rolled her eyes at his exaggerated antics.

"You know I am too." Mike cleared his throat, drawing her attention to the lump of emotion he struggled to swallow around, making Morgan wonder what it would be like to see such awe on her husband, Joe's, face. "It scares me a little, that's all. A baby is so tiny already. So delicate. The thought of a girl half as beautiful as you and the hell I'll have keeping her safe from teenaged horn-dogs..."

James snorted and clasped his middle. "Oh, karma. Gotta love that bitch."

"Seriously, though..." Mike squinted down at his wife, who rubbed her rounded belly in cathartic circles. "What made you say that?"

"I don't know." Kate practically glowed, despite her shrug. "I just...have a feeling. And I keep dreaming about her. I see you sitting there in the corner, on a white rocking chair with a frilly pink cushion, holding our daughter while she sleeps. It feels so real."

Mike set the roller in the tray and crossed to his wife. He wiped his hands on his pants before cupping her cheeks in his trembling fingers. "You saw her?"

"Yeah." Tears tracked down the slightly puffy cheeks of Morgan's best friend. "Both of you together, and knew I could never be more in love."

Morgan couldn't stand upright another moment. The precious outfit she'd crumpled in her fist fluttered to the floor as her fingers went numb. She realized Kate didn't intend for every word to eviscerate her as viciously as if she'd slashed Morgan with a thousand paring knives simultaneously. Still, the ragged cries clawing at her vocal cords threatened to rip free of her throat if she didn't escape the reminder of all she'd never have.

She squeezed past the couple, lost in each other.

When Kate's full abdomen brushed Morgan, she flinched as if scorched. The drop cloth twisted around her foot and she stumbled. Joe reached for her. She couldn't bear to look her husband in the eye, afraid he might recognize her pain. Never would she add to his burdens.

Except it seemed even without intending to, she had. Their relationship had grown strained lately. The more she tried to protect him, the more he seemed to blame himself, and today was no different.

"I'm sorry, Mo," his ragged whisper chased her as she fled the scene of adorable bliss.

Lousy friend.

Horrible partner.

Failure of a wife.

"Morgan." Mike's command boomed from the top of the stairs she clattered down. "Stop. Right now. You're going to hurt yourself."

Something in her obeyed the foreman instinctively. Still, she couldn't force herself to turn and face him. Ashamed, she dashed tears from her cheeks with the heels of her hands. Before she figured out what direction to go next, strong arms surrounded her, lifted her.

She scrunched her lids closed and buried her face in the chest supporting her, too broad to be her husband's or Mike's. Definitely too big for James or Neil. "Dave."

"I've got you, doll." The gentle giant had reached her first. He carried her into the living room where she soon found herself surrounded by friends and lovers.

At times like this, she couldn't have been more certain the crew had evolved into something beyond a gang of friends who doubled as fuck buddies. These eight people—five construction workers and the women they'd made their life partners—shared a bond stronger than sex.

When she peeked from the shelter of Dave's embrace, her gaze locked on her husband as if drawn by a rare-earth magnet. The rest of the group closed rank around them, shuffling Joe to the center of the semi-circle flanking the couch.

Hands guided him, pressing on his shoulders until he sank beside her.

Acid ate holes in her stomach when he sat, stiff. Leaning away from her, he was careful not to touch a single molecule of her legs, bare beneath the hem of her flirty sundress.

"Enough." Mike shattered their perpetual cycle of guilt, pain and self-loathing. "This is insane. I refuse to watch two of my best friends ruining the most amazing thing in their lives. Dave, give her back to Joe."

When the big man kissed her forehead and shifted to transfer her, Joe sighed. "I'm not sure you should force her, Mike. I wouldn't want me either. I'm defective. Useless."

Then no one needed to prod her.

Morgan launched herself at her husband. In her peripheral vision, she caught a glimpse of Kayla hugging Dave, since her mate had been left empty-handed. Morgan and Joe weren't the only ones suffering. Their agony and disappointment radiated outward, tainting everyone who loved them.

How selfish had she been?

"Joe." She straddled his lap. Still he refused to lift his stare from his limp hands. They rested, palms up, on the cushions beside his powerful thighs and her pale knees. "Please, look at me."

When he granted her request, the torment in his stare stole her breath. Ten times more potent than the loss and regret she harbored because he couldn't get her pregnant, his misery ripped her heart from shreds into tatters.

"I'm so sorry," they murmured in unison.

A multitude of hands rubbed Morgan's back and Joe's arms, which banded around her. She spied her friends stroking her husband's powerful shoulders from either side of him, where they had crowded beside and behind the couple on the couch.

"You have nothing to apologize for. *Nothing*. You hear me?" Morgan shook her man, though he barely budged.

"Sure, right. Then why are you pulling away from me?" The laugh lines at the corner of his eyes had all but vanished from disuse. Tension drew them tight, repurposing them into deep gouges in the planes of his usually affable visage. "You can't even bear to be in the same room as me most of the time. I don't remember the last night I fell asleep with you in my arms, or woke to you snuggled next to me. You think I don't know you're stalling when you're downstairs baking until two in the morning? Napping on the couch for a few hours before preparing for the early rush? This is bullshit. I can't take anymore. Just cut me loose already. I can't survive another day wondering if it's the last. The one when you finally admit you deserve better. This resentment is going to poison everything we shared. I don't hold it against you. I understand, cupcake. I can't give you what you need."

Her guts roiled.

She jerked as if he'd slapped her.

And still she wished she could flay herself a million times over for giving him the wrong impression. All that time suffering alone, for nothing.

"No." She smothered his face with butterfly kisses. "You have it all backwards. It's me that's the problem. I'm greedy. Selfish. So angry at myself. How can I be disappointed when I'm so damn lucky?"

"What?" Joe blinked up at her as if she'd lost her marbles.

"I tried to keep busy so you wouldn't see my grief. I didn't want to hurt you." She sobbed. "I think I made a big mistake."

"Shush, both of you." Mike plopped beside them. He nudged the couple with his shoulder, rocking them with his gentle pressure, and infusing them with his heat. "No one is winning here. I let this go on too long. I think because I felt like shit, knowing Kate and I have what you want. I let that fuck with my perspective. This is nuts. You love each other. Nothing should matter more than that."

Morgan glanced up to see Devon, James and Neil nodding their agreement.

Dave stood with his feet spread, his arms crossed over his chest.

"Is this some kind of intervention?" She attempted to deflect the concerned disapproval with levity. Her attempt flopped.

"I guess you could say that." Kate mirrored her husband, sitting on the couch on Morgan and Joe's other side. She cleared her throat, then scanned the gathering. No one spoke up when she paused, so she continued, "We've discussed the matter."

"Who's *we*?" Joe tensed again beneath Morgan. She rubbed his chest, reminding him the crew meant well. "All of you? Talked about us behind our backs?"

His cheeks flamed.

"There was nothing sinister about it," Mike growled. Rare displeasure rolled off the foreman, making Morgan blink. "If I didn't know how rocky these past few months have been, I'd kick your ass for thinking such stupid shit. We're trying to help."

"Oh yeah, and how do you propose to do that?" Joe harrumphed. "Wave your *magic wand* over my cock? Implant some healthy swimmers in my nutsack when I'm sleeping?

They said the chance is next to nothing. No hope, Mike. None. Not all of us can be Captain Fertility like you, knocking up your wife on the first try."

"Don't you see...?" Kate tilted her head, curious yet stern. She would make one hell of a mom.

"See what?" The hairs dusting the nape of Morgan's neck began to rise. She shifted her stare from one friend to the next.

"Dev, grab the folder from the sideboard, would you?" Mike gestured with his chin.

The cute construction worker, the only girl on the crew, dashed for the requested item and delivered it to Mike's outstretched hand in a flash. She smiled softly, then squeezed Joe and Morgan's linked fingers.

When had that happened? Morgan wasn't sure, but she'd missed the warmth of his partnership recently. Only herself to fault for that, really.

"What's all that?" Joe's hostility morphed into curiosity.

"*We* have a surprise for *you* this time." Mike flipped open the manila cardstock and thumbed through the papers inside. "Me, Dave, James and Neil all got tested. You know, for genetic markers and a bunch of other shit I didn't understand much about."

"Why?" Joe squawked. His body vibrated beneath Morgan.

She smothered him with affection as best as she knew how. Because surely, there was only one reason the guys would subject themselves to that kind of medical scrutiny.

Mike looked to his wife for help. Fancy talk had never been his strength. Morgan felt pretty sure what they were about to say might change all of their lives forever.

"They wanted to see which of them would have the best shot of giving you a baby." Kate stuck to direct yet sympathetic. "We also did a lot of research on adoption. We've scraped together some money if you'd rather try that route. But lots of people use sperm banks. You wouldn't have to stick with our guys if the idea makes you uncomfortable. We just thought...you might want some options."

"And you're all willing to make a charitable donation, is that what you're saying?" Joe sneered. "Great, I love being the dude all my friends pity."

"Quit being so defensive." Mike socked him in the shoulder. "This isn't the Joe I know. Pull your head out of your ass and think about this for a second. Look at what you're doing to your wife. Your marriage. Are you willing to throw that all away for pride? If so, then you're not the man I thought I respected enough to suggest this to."

When Joe's stare winged to her, Morgan tried not to flinch. She took a deep breath and held still, afraid to tend the seed of hope Mike had just planted. If it sprouted then withered, she might not survive. Blank, she allowed Joe to form his own impressions.

"Oh, fuck." His head crashed to the cushion behind him. "You're right."

"It's not too late to fix things." Kate finger-combed his hair from his brow. "Tell her what's in your heart. Right now, before the moment's gone."

Joe took a breath so deep his lungs rattled. He sat upright, pressing close. For the first time in months, he donned the confident, sexy swagger he'd always worn as well as his favorite ripped old pair of jeans. "I never want to see that guarded look on your face again, Mo. That's not the girl I love. I can't believe I've done this to you. To us. There were other ways. Other choices. I just... I felt so much like I'd let you down."

"Leave the past alone." Mike kept them on track. "You can only change the future. Where do you want to go from here?"

"Who had the best chance?" Joe didn't hesitate.

"Neil." Mike's smile turned wry. "Apparently, he's pretty lucky he hasn't done it by accident at this rate. Dev should probably double the dosage of her birth control shots."

"You're welcome." James pinched his longtime lover on the ass. Devon, James and Neil laughed as they hugged each other. "Seems like my ass might have saved yours."

"Okay." Joe nodded before returning his gaze to Morgan. "What do you say? Want a tall, pain-in-the-ass kid with blond hair? I bet Neil can rub one out in the doctor's office in thirty seconds or less and we can be on our way. No muss, no fuss, right, Mikey?"

"Something like that." Their foreman sounded wary. "It doesn't have to be so crude."

The clinical nature of the deed frightened Morgan. She imagined bright whitish-blue lights, doctors poking and prodding her, and antiseptic smells corroding what should have been one of the happiest moments of her life. Suddenly she didn't know if she could sign up for such a sterile origin for her child. Then again, what choice did she have?

The pressure of her friends' regard bore down on her until she thought she might be squished flatter than a pancake. They were trying to help. Offering a solution.

"Morgan?" Joe narrowed his eyes as he observed her pulse speeding in her neck.

She had to escape their scrutiny. She couldn't hide anything from the crew. But she didn't know if she was ready to be totally honest yet—either with them...or herself.

"I..." No matter how many times she swallowed, she couldn't manage to clear the lump in her throat. "Thank you. Really. I just... It's a lot. Need some time. To think."

Scrambling off Joe's lap, she rushed for the door.

Heavy booted footsteps trailed close behind her. Their owner didn't try to stop her, but followed at a safe distance instead.

By the time she'd run to the passenger side of Joe's truck, she'd calmed enough to lift her head. Through two panes of glass and the chasm of the cab between, she watched her husband monitoring her reaction. "Let's go home, Mo. We can figure it out together."

The truck separating them distorted his reassurance. Still, she could decipher the movement of his lips. Not hard to understand him. After all, it was as though he read her wishes straight from her soul. If nothing else, she promised him silently right then, she'd quit letting this baby fiasco ruin their relationship.

No matter what she had to do, she'd fix things.

For them both.

Joe climbed inside. He reached across the bench seat to unlock and open her door. Then he extended a green-speckled hand, which she latched on to as if it were a lifeline, and used it to tug her into the vehicle. Without letting go, he backed out of the driveway. His fingers never abandoned hers, not even to wave to the cluster of seven worried friends huddled on Kate and Mike's porch.

She stared at the rest of the crew until they were specks in the side mirror, wondering—with each foot of distance that they added between them and their friends— if she'd dug this yawning pit deeper than it had already been.

CHAPTER TWO

Morgan didn't object when Joe told her to sit tight before jogging around to her side of the truck. She slid willingly into his open arms when he invited her. All her energy had drained away as she mulled over their options on the short ride home. She clutched the manila folder he handed her to her chest and allowed him to carry her up the stairs to their apartment over her bakery, Sweet Treats.

He didn't pause to check the mail or snag some of the leftovers from yesterday's special. Instead, he marched directly to their bedroom and settled her on the bed. Deft fingers swiped her sneakers from her feet, then tucked her beneath the thick strata of covers they preferred.

Joe joined her moments later, gathering her to his chest.

"Mo."

"Joe." They initialized conversation at the same instant. She giggled. "I never noticed before that we rhyme."

"Me either." He grinned, then trailed a knuckle along her cheek. "Guess it's no surprise, though. We were meant to go together. I still believe that."

"So do I." A wince tugged at her lips. "I'm so sorry I let you think otherwise."

"It's in the past." He angled his chin toward the papers clasped between them. "Let's work on the future."

Morgan worried her lip between her front teeth.

"Their offer obviously upset you." He traced the shell of her ear, tucking loose strands of hair off her face. "Why don't we start with why? Do you not want a child if it can't be conceived the traditional way?"

"No. That's not the problem." She shook her head, pushing up a little with one palm on his chest so she could meet him eye to eye. "I admit I hadn't thought of alternate arrangements after they told us it wouldn't be successful to implant your sperm in me artificially. But it's not like I haven't embraced some unconventional practices in the past few years."

"No one's questioning that, cupcake." Joe smiled, then nuzzled their noses together.

"Especially after the shit your ex pulled on you, I'm still amazed you gave me and the crew a shot. Grateful every day that you were brave enough to try again."

"Thank you for being so patient with me." She stared into his warm, dark eyes.

"So if it's not that you object to…" He spoke slowly, as if selecting each word carefully. "You think there could be issues with asking one of the guys to do the job?"

A cringe compressed her spine at his blunt description of what should be a miraculous event. "It does worry me that we'd be risking an awful lot. Let's say Neil did…*donate*. What if he can't let go? What if he wants a deeper relationship with the baby? How will we all feel about that? You, me, Devon and James. Will we be able to cope?"

"Shit. That's a good question." Joe sighed. "I didn't really think of it that way. I know the three of them aren't interested in kids. How many times have they told Katiebug they're glad to spoil her baby temporarily, as long as they get to give it back?"

They both chuckled at the memory. The trio had promised to adore their honorary niece or nephew—though of course they'd said niece—lavishing her with obnoxious toys and hopping her up on sugar before returning her to her parents.

"That's what they've said, but Devon is young. She could change her mind yet. And what if it hurts her to see her husband's child raised as someone else's?" The familiar sting of tears prickled Morgan's eyes. "I couldn't stand to injure one of them just to appease my own desires."

"We can talk to them, double check they're certain." Joe tipped her face toward his. "But I know my friends. They don't say or do shit they don't mean. You can bet Mike and Kate had these discussions with them long before they agreed to hand us that folder. They wouldn't risk disappointing us by rescinding an offer like that."

"And if they're not sure. Really, *really* sure, we can look at adopting." Morgan picked at a string on the edge of the duvet. "It's just so expensive. And it won't be fast. I thought maybe in a few years, when Sweet Treats was more stable and we weren't reinvesting all the profits in growth, maybe then... This gift from the crew is more than we can accept."

"Can I be real honest, Mo?" Joe levered up onto one elbow and leaned his forehead on hers. "I'll do whatever makes you happy, I swear. But if it can't be me who gives this to you... It feels right to have it be one of the crew. They're closer than brothers. More than friends. They're part of me. And if one of them can do this, it's almost like I did in some fashion. Easier to be excited about than if a stranger were to be mixed with you. Though I swear to you, I will love any child we raise together. I swear I'll be the best dad I can be. The best husband and friend."

"I know." She didn't hesitate to grant him reassurance. His decency and commitment were qualities she'd never had reason to question. "Even when I've treated you horribly these past few months—been so self-absorbed, I'm ashamed of myself—you never once wavered. I love you, Joe. And if this is the path you prefer, I'll walk it. I'm so thrilled they offered, humbled really. It's just..."

Panic chilled her as she thought of cold steel tables and instruments beeping in the background instead of warm embraces, flickering candlelight and the soft sighs of great sex. It was a ridiculously small thing to endure. And when they came home, Joe would make love to her. It would be easy to convince herself the magic had happened then.

"That." Joe zeroed in on her reaction as if she'd advertised her discomfort on the Times Square JumboTron instead of attempting to mask it. She could conceal nothing from him. "There it is again. What was that hesitation?"

"It's silly." She shook her head.

"Nothing is trivial if it affects you or our family." Joe flashed the steely core he seldom unveiled. "Tell me what you were thinking just then."

She breathed in, then released the air in a steady stream.

"You can share anything with me. Don't you believe that?" Pain darkened his eyes, drawing his brows lower on his handsome face.

"Yes, of course." Morgan refused to hurt him anymore. "It's just that those procedures are so *sterile*. Formal. Surrounded by strangers. It's not how I would choose to create a new life. I wish it could be borne of our shared joy and pleasure. Instilled with all the love and hope and gratitude I feel when we're together."

"Oh." He sat up, leaning his shoulders against the headboard. "I guess I didn't think that far ahead, cupcake. When you put it like that..."

"It's ridiculous. So many other couples have done the same. If anything, our child will know how much we fought to have him or her in our life. No accidents here." She patted his chest as he stared into the bathroom he'd remodeled for her. The blue and white of the custom handles infused color and style to the small space. "We'll do this our way, however that turns out to be."

"What if—"

"Yes?" She prodded as she enfolded his hand in hers. "Finish your thought."

"We already share." Joe faced her, determination and a wicked smile on his lips. "No reason we can't get you pregnant the old-fashioned way. Just not by me."

"Are you saying...?" Morgan shivered, every pore of her body opening to the idea. Heat flooded her where chill had seeped in before.

"Uh-huh." He nodded. "I'm gonna go out on a limb and say none of the other guys will object. Their ladies either, since we all agreed to be each other's birthday presents. No reason we can't all try together. Would that make it special enough for you?"

"Hell yes." A wave of excitement rolled over her. "I wonder if they'd really be okay with that?"

"Why don't we call a crew meeting and find out?" Joe tugged her over until she straddled him. "As soon as we celebrate our kickass friends and genius brainstorming session. I've missed you a hell of a lot, Morgan."

"Same goes." The kiss they shared started out slowly and gently. Her lips grazed his smile. Settling onto his lap more fully, she ground against his erection, plastering herself to his torso so she could revel in the beat of his heart, which resonated through her chest.

"No matter what happens, we'll always sort it out if we're willing to work together." He murmured against her neck, "I'll never give up on us. On this. I swear."

***

Two weeks after the painting party, Morgan hovered at the edge of her closet, a discarded pile of not-quite-right outfits littering the floor. Maybe the lavender skirt and rich purple sweater Kayla had given her for Christmas would be appropriate.

"Mo, what's the holdup?" Joe paused in the middle of their bedroom. "You're changing? Again? Cupcake..."

"Ug. I know." The thud of her palm smacking her forehead didn't do much good. "It's not like I'm going to be wearing this for very long. I guess I'm pretty nervous."

"I'm not." His smile spread, slow and wide. "I have the easy part. Just watch and wait. Maybe snag a blowjob in the meantime. Way better than shitty coffee in a Styrofoam cup at a clinic or something."

The strained laugh she surrendered only highlighted her tenseness.

Joe crowded behind her, bundling her into his arms so her back rested on his chest. His chin perched on her crown. "You know I'm yanking your chain, right? Well, maybe not about the BJ part. I'm not going to be able to resist when I see you unravel for the crew as usual. Everyone was in favor. Pretend it's your birthday. That you're getting your present a couple months early. If all goes according to plan, you might not enjoy it quite as much then."

The crew had voted to allow each member to be the centerpiece of their libertine sessions, all pleasure focused on them, for their birthday. Helping Dave and, a few weeks later, James indulge in their annual decadence had been highlights she wouldn't soon forget. Somehow, all the power of their attraction focused on her seemed a little more intimidating.

Pressure built as she considered the possibility they wouldn't be successful tonight. What then? Would they have a rematch? How many orgies would it take? After nearly a year of trying to conceive, she worried Joe's condition wasn't the only factor inhibiting their success.

"I can practically hear the gears spinning in your mind. Stress isn't going to help, you know?" Heat combatted some of her chill when Joe's palms traversed her bare arms. "Your ovulation thingy said the timing is right. The setting is right. The people, the love, the intent—everything about this feels fucking perfect. So relax. Enjoy. That's all you have to do. No worries. Come on, now. How about this? I love this color on you. So pretty."

Joe selected the exact ensemble she'd considered. A sign, she thought.

She pivoted in his grasp, wishing she were tall enough to nail him to the wall and kiss the shit out of him. Instead, she settled for wrapping her hands around the back of his neck and encouraging him to bend. She almost forgot about the clothes, the crew and their plans for the evening when they exchanged a fierce yet seductive kiss.

"That's better." He nipped her lip before separating them.

"Maybe we should take the edge off before we go?" Morgan squeezed the thick shaft distorting the crotch of his jeans.

"I think I like you a tad desperate." He cupped her breast in his palm, smirking when she rubbed against his hold like a cat on the corner of a coffee table. "Get dressed. We're leaving in five minutes."

It took her less than three to change into the luxurious fabric, then check her hair and makeup. No sense in delaying any longer. Joe whistled when she emerged into their living room. He swooped in for another kiss, not caring that she'd slathered on a layer of gloss.

"Gorgeous."

"Thank you." The jacket he held out to her slipped easily over her clothes. "I feel like I'm going to a wedding. It all seems so...pivotal."

"It is." Joe kissed her cheek. "I got you something to remember tonight by."

"What?" She glanced up at him, her eyes widening. "You don't know yet if it'll work. Maybe we shouldn't jinx it."

"I'm certain." After fishing in his jacket pocket, he withdrew a tiny velvet box. "I saw it, and I knew you were meant to have it. Tonight is the start of a new era in our lives. I'd like you to wear this, carry something of mine with you."

A gasp escaped her when he flipped the lid open. A dark purple gem set in swirled silver wire winked up at her in the light from their kitchen chandelier. A thin chain ran through a tiny heart at the top of the pendant.

"The jeweler told me amethyst and moonstone are good luck for women trying to conceive. Balances feminine something or other. Not sure I believe that, but I thought it

35

was pretty and it reminded me of you. Can't hurt, right?"

"Right." Tears pooled in her eyes. His genuine and thoughtful surprises always made her day. He couldn't show her in more ways how much he loved her. She'd never felt so valued in all her life as when he was near.

"Joe, I need you to understand." She waited until he finished latching the clasp so it held his gift around her neck. "Even if this doesn't work out. If we never have a child...you are enough for me. You're more than I have a right to hope for."

Raising her knuckles to his lips, he dusted soft kisses there before linking their fingers and guiding her from their home. "I want to give you everything."

"You already have." She squeezed his hand as he boosted her into the truck, tucked her inside, then shut the door carefully.

They rode to Kayla's resort in contented silence, their hands joined again as soon as he took his place behind the wheel. By the time they bumped through the woods, along the twisted path that led to the secluded property hosting Kayla and Dave's house as well as their naturist retreat, stars dotted the sky like glitter set on fire.

She expected Joe to take the fork to the right, which led to the private cabin where their friends lived and most of the crew's interludes took place. Instead, he veered left. Toward the cute bungalows the crew had recently expanded on in response to the initial success of Kay's venture.

Several of them hadn't even opened to guests yet.

Morgan didn't ask where they were going. She trusted Joe to take her where she needed to be. As long as he was by her side, it didn't much matter where they ended up. Good thing her faith in him thrived. The truck slowed in the middle of nowhere until they rolled to a stop in the center of the rustic road.

When he removed a strip of black silk from his back pocket, she knew what he expected. Her lashes rested against her cheeks as she closed her eyes, leaning toward her husband.

"Sweet girl." He fastened the fabric around her head tight enough that she couldn't peek even if she'd tried to open her eyes, yet loose enough to be comfortable.

"For now." The hint of naughty she added to her response had the desired effect.

Joe's voice turned husky. "I like you spicy too."

The anticipated kiss she craved never arrived. The truck started off down the road.

She threw her hand out, searching for the handle on the door or the edge of the seat. Joe's fingers landed high on her thigh. "I've got you."

"I know."

"Almost there." He crooned to her in soft, steady murmurs, never letting her forget he sat by her side. "I see lights now. And there's the crew. They're waiting for you."

"For us."

"True, for us." After a quick squeeze, his hand abandoned her leg long enough to unfasten her seatbelt. "Go with Dave. I'm right behind you."

Before she could respond, the truck door opened. Huge hands engulfed her waist. She floated into their grasp. "You look really nice tonight, Morgan."

Thank goodness she hadn't worn a dress with a short skirt or she'd be flashing her ass to the entire forest. Not that the eight people she couldn't see but knew were there hadn't gotten an eyeful of every inch of her already. Soon they'd be doing a whole lot more than looking too.

Dave's boots thudded on what sounded like wooden treads as they ascended together. The new buildings had adorable porches complete with swings. That must be where they were. She hadn't observed the progress personally, though Joe had told her the crew had decided to take a couple weeks off before starting their next project to help Kay out.

Someone cursed softly. A subtle creak made her sure they'd opened a door for her and Dave. "So sexy, Morgan."

"Thank you, James."

"I'm going to set you down." Dave murmured to her as he lowered her feet to the floor. He braced her shoulders. Scuffles and whispers surrounded her as her friends all assembled as they saw fit. "Joe's got you now."

The big man's hand swapped out for her husband's familiar grasp. Dotted kisses at her temple had her sighing while he worked the knot on her blindfold loose. A steady white noise piqued her curiosity. What could that be? "Tonight is special. For all of us. We wanted you to know how much. Live in the moment, Mo. Take what we're giving."

He whipped the silk from her, letting it slither to the floor unnoticed.

Blinking against the sudden light, she tried to focus. When she did, a sheen of tears immediately turned the flickering candles into glittering sparkles, dazzling her. She reached out. Joe held one hand while Dave collected the other.

"You did all this for me?" The whisper cut through the hush of her eight best friends, who awaited her reaction. Behind the naked, oiled men who stood shoulder to shoulder and their wives—adorned in gossamer togas that hid the bare essentials, proclaiming their intent to sit the festivities out—sheer panels of iridescent fabric draped from exposed wooden rafters.

Zillions of tiny clear lights, like the ones hugging their tree at Christmas, hung behind the soft falls. She felt as though she'd taken up residence in an enchanted snow globe, or maybe a cloud way, way out in some ethereal paradise on the edge of the universe. Romantic touches overflowed the space. Pale silk flowers, warm vanilla candles on wrought iron stands and the largest canopied bed she'd ever seen were just a few of the details bombarding her senses.

"We did it for both you and Joe." Kate smiled from her post with a fluffy white towel draped over her forearm. What the heck?

The guys stepped aside, chiseled bodies parting like a fleshy curtain at the most alluring opera she'd ever attended. Behind them, a waterfall trickled from what could have been a loft. A tiny stream bounced next to vines that looked as real as the ones Kayla had cultivated in the gardens outside. Maybe they were.

Splashes drew her eye from expertly crafted faux stone to faux stone until droplets rained into an elaborate whirlpool fashioned from river rock on the outside and something natural yet smooth-looking in the basin. A gradual slope led up to the dais supporting the magical indoor pond. Lush greenery surrounded the pool. She suspected the window on the other side would grant glorious views of the lake if it were daytime.

A fireplace made from the same cut stone chased away any chill emanating from the glass.

"Whoa." Nothing more elaborate formed in her mind.

Awestruck, she allowed Joe to manipulate her, stripping her sweater over her head and freeing her from her lacey bra before she'd recovered. Next he slid her skirt from her hips, then lifted her from the puddle of gorgeous fabric. He swiped her shoes from her feet and patted her bare ass. No need to remove underwear. She hadn't bothered with panties.

"Nice touch, Mo."

She grinned over her shoulder at her husband. "Glad you approve."

"Now run along and play." A gentle shove inspired her to put one foot in front of the other, heading in the direction of the crew.

"You're not joining us?" She paused.

"Told you." Mike put his hands on his hips. The motion drew Morgan's gaze to his stiff cock, which jutted from the shadow of his trimmed hair. "You can catch up. Wouldn't dare let our girl get a chill waiting for you to undress."

The foreman took a few steps forward, extending his arm as though they really were out for a ritzy night on the town instead of embarking on a procreational interlude of sordid proportions.

"Whatever you're thinking, I don't like it," he hissed. "You got that look. You know the one. Quit it."

A laugh bubbled up from somewhere beneath her nerves. It reminded her of the water in the spa and how it seemed to effervesce from an unknown source. "Yes, sir."

"That's better." He grunted as he led her up the incline then into the water, one step at a time. Miniature waves sloshed against her ankles, then her shins, then her knees. Warm and silky—probably loaded with rejuvenating minerals, if she knew Kayla— the bath felt heavenly. "We figured you might go a little

Type A on us, so we decided to help you relax a bit."

"So far it's working." Tension drained from her muscles as she settled into the seat he directed her to. Water flowed around her shoulders, encouraging her to lean her head back against the contour of the tub, which provided a perfect rest.

"Good." Mike sat next to her. He massaged her hand then her arm until her eyelids fluttered closed. It shouldn't have surprised her when someone took up a similar exploration on her opposite side. Soon after, a third pair of sure fingers cupped her foot, kneading the pad beneath her toes.

She couldn't help but moan.

Finally another set of hands plucked her other foot from the waves and echoed the caresses. A smile tugged at her mouth. Joe's four crewmates pampered her.

"Yeah, lift up one sec. Now lay your head here." Kayla guided her to a folded towel at the edge of the hot tub.

Morgan opened her eyes, reassured to see her friend, upside down and above her. The affectionate smile ensured Kayla didn't begrudge Morgan her indulgence. The women kneeling on either side of Kay grinned too.

"You're doing great." Kate patted her shoulder.

"And I love your necklace. It suits you." Devon nodded.

Morgan wondered if she imagined the heat that seemed to pulse from the pendant where it nestled in the hollow of her collarbones. "Thanks. All Joe, as usual."

Further conversation became impossible when Kayla dipped her fingers in the warm water then laid them on Morgan's cheeks. She began a massage that leeched stress, which Morgan hadn't realized she'd harbored, from her facial muscles. Kayla's gift for soothing others impressed her, as always. Masterful, complex motions loosened every last holdout of tension.

The guys progressed from her extremities to her core, their continuing massage lessons with Kayla evident in their handling. Morgan was glad for their support. Otherwise, she might have drifted away on a swirl of fragrant mist.

"I think she's ready." Kayla spoke low and gently. "The switch is behind you, Joe."

"What—?" Morgan didn't have a chance to finish her question.

With a low rumble, the pattern of the jets in the tub changed. Where they'd been unfocused and random before, several direct flows added impact to the gentle swirl of fluid. Paired columns of water focused on the muscles flanking her spine. A few more pummeled the cheeks of her ass, digging deep into the muscles there to eliminate any knots. Finally, a burst fluttered over her pussy in a maddening oscillation that aroused her instantly.

"Ohmigod."

"Works as advertised, I guess." Dave chuckled from her side. He skipped along his path up her left arm to pet her belly a few times.

"They say having orgasms increases the likelihood of conception." Mike nibbled on her earlobe. "Have no idea if that's a fact. Figured we should give it a whirl just to be safe."

In unison, each of the men rubbing her limbs advanced, stroking her calves, knees, forearms and elbows. She lifted her head, pleased to find Joe had joined them, and was rewarded with a vision of him rising from the steamy water like Neptune, his hand stroking slow and sure over his generous erection.

"No peeking." Kayla draped a washcloth over Morgan's eyes and returned her head to its reclined position, continuing to heighten the sensual trance the men were working her into. "Don't you worry. Your guy is right here. He can't stop staring at you."

"Want him." It didn't matter to her that the statement sounded a bit like a whine given the erotic luxuries her friends lavished on her.

"We can make room." James shifted the angle of her leg. Neil mimicked the motion, splaying her wider, granting the jet more direct access to her swollen pussy.

Joe braced his hands on her thighs, lighting up her nerve endings with his comforting touch. His torso nudged her legs apart as he settled between them, probably kneeling in the deeper water beyond the ledge her ass rested on.

His hand glided across her pussy, making her shriek and squirm. The touch poised her on the edge of orgasm, far too soon. "Wow. The current is pronounced. It's rippling across my hand."

"That's not all it's doing." She gritted her teeth.

"Don't tense up." The pads of Kayla's thumbs prodded Morgan's jaw until she turned pliant once more.

"Or fight us." Mike had progressed to her shoulder. His fingers teased the top swell of her breast. "Feel free to come as often as you like. This isn't some starvation diet."

Kayla's hand seemed cool in the wake of the flush that raced across Morgan's cheeks. She couldn't believe how quickly they'd revved her up. Her ridiculous objections earlier dissolved in the warm water steeped with the care of her friends. If she could have hugged each and every one of them right then, she would have.

"Time to get serious, boys," Devon called out to her mates. They advanced, walking their fingers up Morgan's thighs, swirling and teasing as they rubbed her down.

"You too, Dave," Kayla encouraged her husband. He matched Mike's fondling, which grew bolder by the instant.

Morgan's abdomen undulated, raising her pussy toward the elusive ripple of the continually evolving current. Just when she thought she'd homed in on it, the spray would change.

"More?" Joe slipped his hand between her lips until he was on the verge of penetrating her. "Does your pussy need to be filled?"

She cried out as he fed her the tip of a finger, then two.

"No worries about that," Neil rasped from where he now rubbed her ass and hip. "Soon enough you'll be stuffed. All of us, Morgan. Have you thought about that? Taking four cocks in your pussy in one night?"

"Five." Mike's tone brooked no argument. "Joe will have her last."

"Damn straight he will." Kate clearly approved, from her dulcet tone. "No matter which of you has the winning swimmer, this child is his. Theirs."

"Ours." Joe and Morgan uttered the promise in unison. She didn't doubt for one second he meant the entire crew. She had too.

She squeezed his fingers with her pussy as he insinuated himself more completely within her. Careful to keep his hand low, he allowed the water to continue to caress her clit. Her toes curled.

"Shit, yes." Joe called out to his buddies. "She's close. I can feel her rippling around my hand. Dave, suck on her nipple."

The whoosh of the big man sinking below the surface was followed in short order by his mouth applying pressure on the tip of her breast. Mike mimicked the action from his post on her other side. The dual sensation—combined with Joe stroking her from the inside out, James and Neil petting her flanks and Kayla massaging her face—crescendoed until Morgan had no chance at resistance.

She capitulated to their care, allowing them to cradle her through an orgasm strong enough to burn away the last vestiges of her nerves and replace them with newborn hunger. Mike and Dave broke the surface of the indoor oasis. They dragged mass quantities of oxygen into their lungs. She felt as if they were breathing for her as she gasped and struggled to force enough air into her body to keep her from passing out with the pleasure they'd imparted.

Joe and Kayla anchored her, keeping her from drowning as her entire body thrashed and spasmed. Mike cupped the nape of her neck to quiet her. His reassurance—in conjunction with the long, loving strokes from the four other guys' hands, which roved across her body—granted her the serenity to maximize her enjoyment.

Dave lifted her fingers to press a kiss to her knuckles and *tsked*. "You're getting all wrinkly. Time to get out, I think."

Her eyes fluttered open, unfocused. Lights flickered in her vision like errant fireflies. Joe kissed her softly before climbing over her. Water sluiced from his lithe frame. The three women nearby rushed to dry him with their plush towels. When they'd done their best, he crouched, arms extended.

Mike and Dave scooped their hands beneath her. They lifted her to her husband. He plucked her from the whirlpool, then held her out for Dev, Kayla and Kate to care for. Softness enveloped her as they rubbed her down.

"Next." Devon winked and moved on to Neil.

"Go ahead, Joe." Mike directed traffic. "Make your wife comfortable. We'll be there in a minute."

CHAPTER THREE

Morgan couldn't believe how completely the crew had transformed a simple cottage into a fairy tale hideaway. Everywhere she looked, touched, something delighted her senses. Yards upon yards of eyelet fabric draped from the rafters, making the space around the bed seem like a cocoon spun of seduction, love and wistful dreams.

Pinned in spots to form a luscious canopy, the airy cloth fluttered in the light breeze circulating through the intimate space, courtesy of the wide-bladed ceiling fan. It spun idly to keep the heat from absconding to the apex of the peaked ceiling. Joe ducked beneath yet more netting, this batch complete with fine silver filaments that coruscated in the glow of the twinkling lights. She trailed her fingers along the gauze as he delivered her to the platform bed.

"This is…" She had no words.

"I know." Joe nuzzled her neck as he settled over her. "When Kayla showed me the design inspiration pictures, I had my doubts she could pull it off. Now, when I see this, it's far beyond what I had envisioned. She's going to keep it staged. A honeymoon suite for the resort."

"Think we could get married a few dozen times?" she sighed.

"That can probably be arranged." Joe pressed a kiss to each corner of the smile she hadn't even realized her mouth had curved into. "I do know the owner pretty well, you know?"

Morgan giggled. "So I've heard."

"And there's so much more yet to come, Mo." Her husband rubbed their noses together, staring deep into her eyes. "Are you ready? Are you sure?"

"Absolutely." She didn't have a doubt left in her mind or heart. "Are you?"

"Hundred percent." He smothered her in a kiss so rich she knew she'd never forget this moment and the connection burning between them. She wrapped her arms and legs around him and returned the fervor of his lips, tongue and teeth.

Morgan didn't acknowledge the shifting of the mattress beneath her until someone pried Joe from her clasp.

"Excuse me. I believe I have this dance." Mike tapped Joe on the shoulder as though he were part of a naughty tag team.

Joe licked his lips. He shook his head, clearing the haze generated when they met soul on soul. *Later,* he mouthed to her while drawing a cross over his heart.

She blew him a kiss.

"You're making me jealous." Mike issued a mock growl. "I get some of that sugar too, right?"

"Of course." Morgan put her arms up and welcomed him into her embrace. Over his shoulder, Joe nodded before he smacked the foreman on the rump.

Mike didn't flinch. Instead, he continued to impress himself on her from his toes to his hot and ready cock to his mouth. He laughed between her parted lips. "Yeah, sweetie, that's all for you tonight."

When he'd slowly and thoroughly delved to the far recesses of her mouth, he retreated enough to rasp into her hair. "Do you realize how much I've dreamt about taking you like this? All the way? It'll be our first time with no condom between us. No diaphragm either. What the hell were we thinking?"

"I don't know anymore. This feels good." She ran her hands up his powerful back, enthralled and appreciative of his presence in her life. She'd been ecstatic when her best friend found this man, and now she got to share in the wealth of rapture and security he provided for Kate, as well as the rest of the crew.

"I'm glad tonight is special for us." He kissed along her brow line. "I hope I can give you what you wish for. If not, I'm still gonna enjoy the hell out of this opportunity to show you how much I respect you and how lucky I think Joe is to have you. We all are. I've hated seeing you both suffer. No more. Only happiness from here on out."

All the while, he touched her. Skilled hands roamed her body—down her ribs, over her face, along the sides of her breasts. When he lifted a tiny fraction, putting minimal space between their torsos, she whimpered.

"Don't worry. I'll take care of you. One second." He brushed his thumb across her damp mouth as he reached for a couple pillows. "We have to make this count, huh? Gravity will aid and abet these little guys in their escape if we're not careful to make you a one-way avenue."

Someone off to the side snorted when he manhandled his junk. "Classy, babe."

"Hey, I am what I am." Mike tossed a wry grin at his wife. "Haven't heard any complaints from you before."

"Never will." Kate had curled up in a divine wingback chair. She slung one arm over her full belly and tucked her feet onto the pad by her ass. "I love you, Mike."

Morgan tried twice to speak when he propped up her hips then sank so that his cock rode the furrow of her pussy. "Kate."

She couldn't bear it if her friend changed her mind later and decided this had been over the line. They'd been BFFs since they'd hidden beneath their bunk beds with a deck of Go Fish cards and a stash of stale Thin Mints to avoid traipsing through mosquito-infested woods at the Girl Scout camp from hell in seventh grade. Wonder if there was a merit badge that covered helping your best friend get pregnant?

That was a lot of history to risk.

Kate leaned forward enough to squeeze Morgan's hand. "It's the right thing for us. Enjoy. Tire him out, would you? I haven't been feeling up to much lately."

Morgan laughed. Mike didn't. She licked the lines of strain bracketing his mouth. "You really are strung tight tonight, aren't you?"

"Yeah. Sorry. I worry when she's not feeling well. And this is a ton of responsibility. Plus, I'm afraid I'm not going to last that long." He scrunched his eyes closed for a moment. "It's been a while. You feel great beneath me.

Soft. Hot. The idea of making a baby...another baby... It's powerful."

He adjusted his hips. With his hands tangled in her hair, he attempted to penetrate using just the motion of their pelvises. Newish to each other, they couldn't quite get lined up right.

"James, give him a hand." Devon coached one of her husbands from a similar chair to Kate's, which sat at the foot of the bed. She must have had one hell of a view despite the three men lounging beyond the tangle of Morgan and Mike's toes. Dave and Neil each rested their shoulders against a bedpost, while James had been cradled with his back to Neil's chest. Kayla sighed from her vantage point at Morgan's right, her thighs splayed over the arms of her matching seat.

"You two are sexy together." She whimpered as she drew circles over the damp crotch of her sheer panties.

Morgan would have responded, except James chose right then to tip forward far enough to insert the head of Mike's cock into her dripping pussy. All three of them strangled groans.

"I'll try to go slow." Mike huffed as though he'd sprinted around the resort a few times.

"Please don't." Morgan clutched his shoulders, aware of her nails sinking into the thick pads of muscle there. "I can't wait either. Been thinking about this for almost two weeks. Damn ovulation cycle."

"Tell me about it," Joe grumbled. "Those months we waited then did it on command a hundred times in a row... I don't know how gigolos do it. I swear my cock was sore afterward."

He stretched out on his side next to the temporary couple, positioning himself so he could peel one of Morgan's hands from Mike and enfold it in his own. He kissed her palm, then held on tight.

"Oh, sure. We feel so damn sorry for you." Kayla kicked him lightly in the ass. "Like you didn't love every moment."

"You know I did," he answered Kay, yet he never deflected his stare from Morgan.

"Me too." She squeezed his fingers tighter than she intended when Mike plunged a bit deeper.

"Damn. Sorry." He cursed below his breath. "You're killing me with all this talk."

"Do it, Mike." Her attempt to wrap her leg around his hip was less than successful given the incline of her torso. Hell, he really had her hiked up. The thought of his come pooling inside her while his friends added to the mix sent a bolt of lightning from her brain straight to her pussy. She clenched around him.

"Not going anywhere when you're tighter than a fist." He attempted to work through her rings of muscle. Soaked, her body still had to be cajoled to permit him entry. "You sure I'm not hurting you, sweetheart."

"Uh-huh." She didn't care that the affirmation held no ladylike grace, only desperate craving. "More."

Mike concentrated then. They all knew when he set his mind to something... Well, you'd better look out. He whipped up his charm along with his persistence, plying her breasts with deceptively tender ministrations while he forced his shaft deep inside her.

Each crewmember fucked differently. They had their own styles. With her eyes wide open, she assembled visual memories she'd snipped while studying him with the other guys—and more recently the women, herself included.

"My favorite thing about you is when you get bossy. You're a natural leader, Mike." She couldn't believe she found her focus long enough to share the admiration in her heart for him. "Your children will have that spark. I would be lucky to foster that brand of bravery."

His stride hitched with him seated almost fully.

"Thank you." He blinked several times as though to clear away the moisture threatening there. "Now stop talking and put that pretty mouth to better use."

Lips descended on hers, preventing her from injecting some smartass remark into the heat of the moment. Honestly, that was more Devon's thing anyway. Morgan preferred to be honest and open in her affections. Mike sucked her bottom lip into his mouth, nibbling on the plumped flesh. The man could kiss, that was for sure. Maybe not with all the finesse of James or the caring of Joe, but with heat and drive and pure passion. *Yes*.

"Do that again." Joe directed Mike. "You just made the muscle in her jaw twitch like it does before she loses it."

What was her husband talking about? She'd have to ask him later. Way later.

"Don't worry. Felt it straight through my cock." Mike rocked inside her, rubbing himself on every swollen inch of her pussy. "You didn't tell me Mo was so submissive. Why haven't I noticed before? You're going to have to let us tie her up soon."

This time she couldn't deny half her face practically seized. How could it not when she clenched her jaw to keep from begging him to try it without hesitation? Every time she shared herself with the crew, she learned more about her inner core—who she really was and who they could be together.

Mike pursued the lead like a pitbull with a juicy bone. He bracketed her wrist, the one not already captured in Joe's hold, and pinned it to the pillow beside her cheek. His hips hammered into her, driving him home to the full extent within her moist channel. She swore she could feel his blunt head tucking directly against her cervix each time he bottomed out.

"You want us to rule you? Make you take what we're giving you? You will because you trust us to love you and bring you only the greatest of pleasure along with a twinge of pain." He uncovered a fantasy she hadn't realized she'd buried. So deep she had never admitted the curiosity even to herself. Maybe she'd never trusted anyone with absolute faith before. "I won't forget, Morgan. How much you like this."

Before she could figure out what he meant, he released her wrist. His hand snaked between them, his fingertips pinching her nipple.

Not gently.

Not brutally.

Just right.

At the same time, he ground himself between her thighs in a sinful figure eight that kept him buried balls deep yet stimulated every possible area of her pussy, inside and out. Her clit mashed against the flat, taut plane of his torso, just above his cock. The veins and ridges of his shaft aggravated the lining of her channel, which fluttered around the embedded cock that nudged, nudged, nudged her in all the right places.

Morgan tried to warn him, but it was no use. She shouldn't have bothered.

"Damn, I can see her coming around you." Dave groaned.

"Better keep your hand off your hard-on, buddy," Kayla chided her husband. "Wouldn't want you wasting the good stuff before it's your turn."

The steady commentary of her friends and lovers spurred Morgan to greater heights. She loved sharing this moment with all of them. At one time, she might have been self-conscious about surrendering so completely before their eyes. Now having them with her only magnified her pleasure. Her orgasm grew in intensity until she would have sworn she would hurt Mike with the force of her clamping.

The strangled cry he emitted seemed to support that theory.

Until the flood of desire rushed out of his cock and poured inside her as thick and hot as a lava flow. He pumped into her in time to the spurts blasting her unprotected pussy. Milking him deliberately, Morgan concentrated on obeying Kayla's calm yet clear instructions for wringing every last drop of semen from his balls.

"Jesus." His arms shook as he held himself up enough to prevent crushing her.

Joe reached out, steadying his friend. When the imminent threat of her being turned into a pancake by a smoking hot construction worker had passed, he petted Morgan with loving caresses, allowing his hand to wander between her and Mike until his fingers ringed his best friend's softening shaft. "Pull out."

The foreman kissed her cheek, then slipped from her body. Pearlescent fluid clung to his cock. She whimpered at the reminder of their purpose.

"Wait." Joe collected the remnants, stroking along Mike's length with his index finger. Mike shuddered and cursed. Dave leaned forward to brace him while Joe finished his thorough cleaning.

"I realize it probably doesn't make a difference." Joe smiled softly when she would have interjected. "Still, I like the idea of you taking it all."

Morgan's eyes rolled back when he spread the lips of her pussy and smeared the thick cream along her opening.

"There, that's better." He hummed his approval.

"I've got to be next." Dave shouldered Mike aside, trusting Neil and James to situate the nearly comatose man in the corner of the bed, propped as Dave had so recently been to ensure he didn't miss a moment of the action. "Unless…"

Dave paused, his hand idly traversing the bold thickness of his erection.

"You're not too much for me." Morgan held her arms up and open again. "I've had you before. You fit me just fine, remember?"

The concern clouding his eyes cleared up in the wake of his smile. "Oh, hell yeah. I thought you might rocket into space the day you rode me in our living room chair, when we all swapped partners."

Blushing was ridiculous. It didn't matter, Morgan's cheeks heated at the reminder of the first time they'd gone round robin with each other. She'd come again and again with hardly any effort, turned on by living out a longtime fantasy and discovering the real thing to be a million times better than her imagination had proclaimed it would be.

"You're cute when you turn shy." He nudged her legs wide enough to accommodate his huge, though fit, frame. Burrowing close, he kissed her softly, then stroked her hair, helping her recover from the ecstasy Mike had inspired while keeping the embers of her desire glowing.

His bulk sheltered her from anything beyond their embrace.

"A child of yours would have a kind and accepting nature. I promise Joe and I will protect the baby, and allow him or her to blossom into a person as generous and loving as you are. It would be an honor." She trailed her fingertips over his ripped muscles. Just because he was stronger than an ox didn't mean he didn't need to be cared for. She would never make that mistake, not knowing him as well as she did.

Joe cleared his throat from beside her. Proving her point, Dave extended his hand and tapped Joe on the cheek, roughly scrubbing over the five o'clock shadow Morgan adored. "I wouldn't trust very many people with my legacy. You know Kay and I aren't planning to have kids of our own, so I hope you don't mind me saying I really pray this works out. I'd like to know some part of me will live on after I check out, and I couldn't think of any better people to nurture that seed than you."

Dave glanced at his wife. She flashed a watery smile in their direction. Neil leaned over to rub her shoulder and she tipped her cheek onto his knuckles. Kayla whispered, "Good luck."

With her blessing, Dave notched the tip of his fat cock in the vestibule of Morgan's pussy. Pressure built. He rocked until the head penetrated, breaching her initial resistance. They both gasped when she hugged his engorged cap.

"I love watching you surrender to him." Joe traced the taut tissue of her inner lips around his friend's intrusion. "It seems impossible, until it's not. It makes me wish I could give you more."

"You've given me everything." Morgan laid her fingers on Joe's chest, over his heart. "Everything that matters. Home, family, friends and your love. What else is there?"

They exchanged an entire conversation with one look. Reassurance she could never find him lacking. Oaths to continue to provide unfailing support for each other, no matter what obstacles the future flung in their paths. All with the security provided by the crew woven throughout. Together they were unbreakable.

She'd nearly forgotten Dave existed as she and Joe locked lips. Or perhaps he simply became an extension of the man she loved. Her husband plied her mouth with tender nips and flicks of his tongue across the sensitive underside of her own, distracting her from the discomfort caused by the advancement of his burly friend. Until Dave bucked and groaned, igniting a conflagration that burned her nerve endings from the inside out.

"Sorry, sorry." He panted, though he froze between her legs, his cock fully impaling her. "It's just, you're so...squishy. Warm and wet. Mike must have been saving that up for a few days."

Kate whimpered, cutting through Dave's awe.

The foreman abandoned the bed. He scooped his wife into his arms and settled himself in the oversized armchair, tucking her to his glistening chest. Reminding Morgan of a horse, steaming in the winner's circle after a mad dash to the finish, tired yet proud, he stroked Kate's hair. "It's fine. I'm a big boy. I can take care of myself. You haven't been feeling well. Concentrate on staying healthy and helping my *son* grow strong. I've got the rest. Hell, it's not like I'm going to be horny for a solid year after tonight."

"Promise?" Kate blinked up at her man.

"Yeah, I'm good. Perfect."

"Shit. Didn't think..." Dave's cock lost some of its steeliness.

"It's impossible to hang on to reason when you're visiting paradise that sweet." James mediated the potential awkwardness, as usual. "I can't wait to feel her for myself. Though after you, I'm afraid I'm not going to be very impressive."

"I've got an idea." Neil whispered in James's ear, pausing to nibble on his lover's lobe.

"You dirty bastard." James shivered. "Pour on the speed, Dave. I'm in a hurry to try this deviant's latest scheme."

Morgan chuckled when Dave looked from guy to guy surrounding them. Distracted, he lost a little of his focus. Kayla unfurled herself from her chair and climbed onto the elevated bed. She sidled up behind her husband and brushed her almost-bare breasts across his back.

Though her hands weren't visible, Morgan could guess what kind of magic they worked when Dave shuddered between her legs. The other woman spoke, low and wicked, to her husband. "Remember what I told you before? How it turns me on to see you lose yourself to giving one of our friends pleasure? How I'm going to reward you later? Too bad I didn't think to bring my strap-on or we could have been a little more efficient. I'm a fan of multitasking."

Dave jerked forward, his cock firming with every pounding beat of his heart. Buried as deep as possible, he inflated within Morgan, stretching her until she swore she'd never been so full in all her life.

Indentations made by Kayla's dark purple nails on Dave's pecs caught Morgan's attention. The prickle they caused only seemed to rile him further. His nostrils flared, and muscles ticked beneath the ink swirling across his olive skin, making him look like a bull ready to charge. His wife waved the red cape of his turn-ons like a world champion matador.

Morgan didn't mind being pierced by his horns.

"There you go." Kayla spanked Dave several times in rapid succession. Morgan imagined flaming handprints appearing on his tight ass. "Give it to her nice and we'll play rough later."

"Looks like Mo isn't the only one exploring lately." Mike raised an eyebrow from his place at the head of the bed.

"Devon gave me the idea." Kay beamed at her friend. She sank onto the arm of Dev's chair instead of returning to her outpost. "I love that we learn from each other. Constant progression. Getting old together will never be boring when we're changing and growing all the time."

Dev patted the cushion beside her hip as she scooted to one side of the oversized seat. Kayla slipped beside her friend, gathering the smaller woman close so their legs braided. She kissed Devon with the soft yet fierce passion the crew had come to expect from the pair on occasion. "Thank you."

"Anytime." Devon winked, then got comfy, resting her head on Kayla's shoulder.

"Oh, shit. They're making out, aren't they?" Dave clenched his jaw. He retreated only long enough to advance again, less carefully this time.

"Shit yeah," Joe teased. "With lots of tongue and even some boob fondling."

"Really?"

Morgan didn't blame Dave for looking over his shoulder. She giggled at the epic pout that crossed his face when he realized Joe was pulling his leg.

"We'll save the show for later. You need to focus." Devon ratcheted up her stern inner minx. She was getting pretty damn proficient at playing the part. "If you do a good job, maybe I'll help Kayla teach you a lesson after we're done here."

"Don't fuck this up." Neil added another swat to Dave's ass. "I want to watch."

"Morgan…" Wide eyes implored her to help.

"Nobody's stopping you." She ran her fingers through his hair. "Fuck me, Dave. You don't have to go slow."

"Want it to be special." His face lowered enough so he could capture her mouth beneath his. The soothing kiss he imparted had little in common with the jacking of his hips. An apology transmitted through every soft caress of his tongue. Tenderness offset by the power of his thrusts between her quivering thighs.

Heat and wonder built inside her like steam in a pressure cooker. Weight compressed her chest as he descended, trying to close any lingering gaps between them. Their perspiration-coated skin adhered where they collided. The insides of her knees stuck on his ribs as he folded her practically in half.

Metal brushed her nipple. The warmed bar of his piercings glanced across her pebbled flesh, inciting a riot in the primed tissue of her breasts. How could he be so tough and yet so sweet? So huge and yet maybe the most delicate of all the men?

Morgan hugged him to her, sheltering him in a welcoming grasp. The discomfort of his oversized cock and heavy body were nothing compared to the bliss of granting him safe harbor and an outlet for the glorious energy he'd obviously pent up.

"It is. Perfect." She encouraged him to abandon the last of his inhibitions by dragging her nails down the bunched sinew on either side of his spine hard enough to leave proof of the claim she staked. Her heels drummed on his ass when he rutted in earnest.

Morgan scooted toward the headboard as he plowed into her, over and over.

Joe shifted, draping one arm beneath her head, around her shoulders, to anchor her through the storm of Dave's unleashed fervor.

She couldn't do more than hang on and enjoy the ride. Tingles spread throughout her body, electrifying her from her fingers to her toes. Focusing on the absolute pleasure, she cultivated the sensation, fertilizing it until it bloomed out of control.

"It won't be much longer." James murmured in the background. "Are you almost ready, Neil?"

"Been waiting our turn for at least nine million years, haven't we?"

"Just feels that way." Mike shushed the pair. "Don't distract Morgan."

As if she could think of anything but the force of the man driving inside her, pushing her tighter to her husband with every surge of precise momentum Dave instilled in her. His scrunched lids flew open, revealing the clear honesty in his bright eyes. "Want this. So badly. Both of you. Deserve it. To have what you need."

The intensity of his desires percolated through every pore of Morgan's body. She absorbed each droplet of the genuine compassion oozing from him while hoping she deserved such gallantry. Her body responded to the emotions barraging her heart and soul. It squeezed him tight, enhancing the effort he dedicated to pleasing her in this moment as well as the greater scheme of their lives.

She hadn't imagined she could come with each man this evening. In the recesses of her mind, she remembered Mike's advice—orgasms improved the odds of conception. Thank God it wasn't the other way around or she'd stand no chance at all.

Her toes curled as ripples began to undulate her swollen channel around the constant invasion of Dave's shaft. Balls slapped against her ass each time he ground deep within her. They both shouted as they escalated each other's pleasure through the natural expression of their own rapture.

"I'm going to come," Dave bellowed. He threw his head back and impressed her all over again with the magnitude of his strength. Muscles twitched as he restricted the range of their flexing.

Morgan looked to Joe. No speech was possible, or necessary.

Greedy. If she was going to climax, she required everything Dave had to give.

"Fuck her harder." Joe spanked Dave. A crack rang through the room as his palm met bunched muscle. "Give her all of you. She can handle it. Wants it. *Needs* it."

The plaintive mewling that erupted from her throat might have been embarrassing if she hadn't been so desperate to shatter with her husband's friend. Instead, the sound seemed to infiltrate Dave's resistance.

Roaring in a primal display she'd never witnessed from him before, Dave grasped her hips, tilted her to optimize the angle of his invasion, then dug deep. He rammed inside her, reaching magical spots she'd only heard clinical discussions about in the past. The fringes of her vision grew smoky as she held her breath in anticipation of the climax about to burst through her.

Flares danced in front of her eyes when she shattered. Though she squirmed and thrashed, Dave never let go. He rode her with the single-minded purpose of a man driven beyond sanity, boundaries or polite considerations. When the clenching of her muscles prohibited him from plunging as fast as he preferred, he locked deep instead.

Intermittent grunts rained over her like the plop of thick cake batter from the wire attachment of her favorite mixer. Dave bit her neck and trapped her. Utterly helpless to move, she was forced to endure every blinding sensation, on the verge of too intense. Too amazing.

And then she felt it.

Scalding heat flooded her pussy.

Dave emptied himself inside her one stream at a time. He jerked in synch with the spasms gripping him, cursing and praising her with every wrenching wave of his orgasm. Their hips banged together at each involuntary buck that enhanced the natural range of his spurts inside her. A wash of liquid lust drenched her.

His climax seemed to last forever, renewing hers with each additional seizure of his muscles and the strangled groans accompanying them. The final two or three pulses of his cock tapered off, leaving him moaning and chanting her name in reverent sighs.

Morgan floated, completely dazed. She tried to cling to his sweaty shoulders when he retreated, but he slipped between her fingers. Strong hands pinned her to the mattress, preventing her from following. "Shh. Don't sit up yet, cupcake."

"Joe."

"I've got you. Stay still. Catch your breath. God, that looked incredible." He kissed her brow so sweetly tears stung her eyes. "You're so gorgeous when you unravel like that."

Half-entranced, she started to roll toward him.

"Keep that ass in the air." Mike's command knifed through the fog in her brain, reminding her of their purpose. How could she have forgotten, even for a moment?

Joe began to rearrange the pillows beneath her hips, enhancing the incline to guarantee the mingled fluids of two of his best friends remained deep in the well of her pussy.

She couldn't say if her whimper had more to do with the thought of their deposits or the ecstasy still gripping her mercilessly or the blinding love her husband inspired or the pressure the awkward angle put on her neck. Probably a bit of each.

"Let me help." James crawled beside her. He motioned with his chin. Neil and Joe complied, lifting her high enough for their lover to worm beneath her body and prop his own pelvis on the feather-stuffed ramp they'd constructed ad hoc. The two men lowered her into the comforting cradle of his mass. James cushioned her while maintaining the optimum angle. The nape of her neck rested comfortably on the curve of his shoulder.

"Much better," she sighed.

"I aim to please." James cupped her breasts. "Plus, this is a great spot for copping a feel."

Morgan laughed, trying to keep her eyes open despite the lassitude barraging her.

The entire bed shook, jostling them all, when Dave crashed—completely limp—onto his face at the foot of the mattress. Kayla and Devon reached out to soothe him with long, smooth glides of their hands. Murmured praise babbled in soft tones Morgan couldn't decipher. She strained for a glimpse of the contented smirk on his face.

"Don't worry about him," Neil flashed his asymmetrical grin. "He'll survive. He just needs some time to recover after that wild ride."

"Me too." She hid her flaming cheeks in the crook of James's neck.

Why did she feel like everything changed by the moment? It was as if her chemical makeup had been irrevocably altered by the radiant emission of their love and the attempts they'd made on her and Joe's behalf.

How could she take more when she'd already been given so much?

"I don't know, feels like your pussy is still begging," James rasped in her ear.

"You're inside me?" She wished she could rescind the question the moment Joe choked at her side. It wasn't that she hadn't felt anything *down there*, but rather that she'd felt too much. Assumed it was an aftereffect of Dave's possession.

"Well, that'll make a guy try harder." James flexed beneath her in a sinuous motion that left no doubt as to the accuracy of his claims.

"Urg." A contented gurgle served as her only reply.

"That's better." His smile warmed his tone. "No hard feelings, love. Dave is huge. I imagine it's hard to discern anything aside from extra happy tingles, considering the way that orgasm looked from where I was sitting."

Dave grunted his agreement, his finger idly drawing swirls over her anklebone from where he splayed.

"So maybe I better do this before she recovers?" Neil knelt between two sets of spread thighs. He looked not at them, but at Joe when he made his suggestion.

"You're the expert at tandem fucking, not me." Joe sat on his haunches, close to her and James's heads as though monitoring her reactions with strict observation and intention to shut down the operation at the slightest hint of trouble.

Morgan didn't pay much attention to their banter. With her eyes closed, she drifted through euphoria, sturdy arms around her and rhythmic breaths lulling her with their metered rise and fall. What could they have in mind? She decided to relax and grant them complete control. Not one fiber of her being lacked trust in them, either singly or as a whole.

"Right." Neil's determination had her prying her lids open in time to catch his grimace. "Hold her tight, boys. She's going to be sensitive at first."

James's arms banded around her waist. Joe cupped her jaw in his hand, angling her face so she met his stare. He crooned encouragement when Neil advanced, sliding into her still-throbbing sheath beside his life partner.

"Ohmigod!" She didn't mean to wriggle, but she couldn't help herself.

"Joe…" Neil paused, checking in with her husband.

"Don't stop, it was a good OMG."

She'd never been so glad he could read her mind. If Neil had changed his course then she'd have wept with frustration. How could they continue to elevate her enjoyment?

Part of the pleasure came from realizing she was a conduit for the two men to love each other. James shivered beneath her as his mate's cock rode along his ultra-firm length. An involuntary flex compressed them within her. The idea of pleasing them both, pressing them together, sent aftershocks racing along her pussy.

"Feel that?" Neil cursed.

"She's still coming." Rough breath stirred the hairs at her temple, tickling her cheek. James simultaneously melted and stiffened beneath and inside her. "From Mike. From Dave."

"All of you." She combed the sheets and covers with a widespread hand until her knuckles knocked into Joe's knee. Unfocused eyes prevented her from reading his expression. When she walked her fingers up his corded thighs and surrounded his impressive erection in her palm, there was no denying how her wanton display impacted him.

Several uncoordinated passes along his length had her frustrated she couldn't maneuver as she pleased. "Come closer."

"Don't have much choice when you tug on it like that. It's not a leash, Mo." His grumble mixed with a chortle.

"Seems pretty effective to me." Kate stuck up for her best friend.

"Let me taste you." Morgan licked her lips, then parted them as she strained her neck toward his bobbing cock.

The brush of his silky head over her mouth had her drawing him inside instinctively. Positioned so that he could feed her his entire length, Joe dangled his balls across James's jaw.

"Help yourself." Neil glided inside her as he encouraged his mate to add the salty tang of Joe's nuts to the stimuli driving him inevitably toward total annihilation.

Another shockwave passed through Morgan when James's full lips met hers at the base of Joe's cock. Abs bunched and released beneath her lower back as he fucked up into her. Each thrust was timed to James laving her husband's delicate sac.

"Oh, shit." Joe's hand tangled in her hair, adding a bite to the gentle massage of his fingertips on her scalp. If James's purr were any indication, he received similar treatment.

"You weren't joking, Dave. She's fucking soaked. Feels so damn good. Slippery." Of all the things Neil had on his long list of personal accolades, stamina had never ranked very high. It seemed he already bordered on the edge. "So slick when I rub over James. He feels like satin inside her. But hard. Fuck. So hard."

Waves of rapture battered Morgan, increasing in frequency and intensity until she couldn't tell where one ended and the next began. The two men shuttling inside her passed each other with each return journey, their counterpoint voyages generating delicious bumps as their heads lodged within her tunnel at different points.

Subtle variations in timing kept her guessing as to when the largest knot of them would form. The combination of their crowns created a bulge that massaged her tensed muscles from within. Joe took advantage of her slack jaw to bury himself to the root. He poked into her throat. She swallowed around him, wishing he could feel even a sliver of the miraculous attention his friends lavished.

"Careful," Mike warned from his post beside them. "Too much more of that and Joe is going to forget to add his load to the rest. Deep inside Morgan. Remember the plan?"

They'd strategized the best way to fuck her tonight?

Morgan couldn't restrain the full-body shiver of delight that coursed through her at that revelation. She wondered what tricks they kept secret in their playbook for another time. Nothing could surpass this moment. Glorious, pure and perfect, she couldn't have loved each of them more.

"Just a minute, Joe." Neil panted as he redoubled his strokes. "Hang on a tiny bit longer. I can't wait. Not much more."

James laughed at the desperation in his lover's declaration. Not out of cruelty, but because he adored the moment the man of his dreams reached fulfillment.

"And you'll be right there with him." Mike reminded James. "You never can resist him coming on you. Sorry, but tonight you're going to have to give up your favorite dessert. Mo gets to keep it this time."

James pulled off Joe's testicles with a slurp. Probably for the best, as her husband's shaft had taken on the defined ridges that proclaimed him ready to explode. "There's always later."

"Ah, God. Yes. Later." Neil shorted the amplitude of his strokes. He fucked fast and furious. The motion declared his imminent breakage. "You. Devon. You'll suck me together. Later."

Before he'd finished issuing the prophecy, Morgan's best chance at conceiving was realized. She hugged Neil to her as tight as she could, given the frantic pace of his fucking. Granting him as much comfort as possible, she clung to him while come jettisoned from his balls.

"Arghh." James turned hard as a stone slab beneath her. He froze, then shouted, "Feel it. Shooting on my cock. Right on the head. Oh. Damn. Right there. Right there."

Then Morgan could no longer discern the individual sensations bombarding her. Two men pumped within her, drenching her folds with their semen. The idea alone, maybe aided by the erratic press of Neil's pelvis bone on her clit, triggered yet another pulse of orgasm in her. Shudders wracked her body.

She must have thrashed hard enough to dislodge James, because next thing she knew, Dave and Mike were helping the longtime pair disentangle themselves from her. Only Joe remained in her field of vision. He fixed her pillows, though she slumped, as floppy as a rag doll wherever he placed her.

"Even like this, I can see their come about to spill from you." He dipped his finger in the pool of thick fluid, then held it out to James, who gladly cleaned the work-roughened digit. "You're brimming with all they've given you. Us. It's as much as we can do."

Morgan tried to lift her hand when his voice crackled. Utterly wrecked, she couldn't.

Mike held Kate in his arms as he stood. He leaned close to Joe to whisper something in his ear. Kate took the opportunity to kiss Joe's cheek. She licked at his cheekbone as though clearing away a rogue tear. Soon Devon, Kayla and their men huddled close. They petted Joe, offering him comfort when Morgan could not.

Each crew member spoke softly to him, rubbing his back, patting his ass, hugging him from behind. And when the flurry of male and female reassurance alike had swarmed over him, he knelt just a little taller between Morgan's thighs. The buzz of affection and praise traveled over her as well.

She closed her eyes, enjoying the soothing of her husband and their seven best friends. And that's when she felt Joe—she'd know him anywhere, no matter how many other lovers she took—press inside her. Careful, gentle and reverent, he fused their bodies.

Her lids fluttered open.

Stares locked. She didn't have to glance around the room to realize they were alone. The crew had left them to bond. To claim the new life she felt sure they had created. Endless disappointments flashed through her mind. Month after month of periods coming to shame her with their failure.

Somehow she knew... Those days were gone.

The universe couldn't be so cruel as to mock the union they'd joined in tonight.

At the heart of everything, was this.

Joe.

"Hi," he whispered against her lips as he moved the barest bit within her tender pussy.

"Hi."

"Not sure where you went just now, but I missed you." Gentle strokes of his fingers through her tangled hair swelled her heart to unimaginable proportions. "Must have been somewhere good to put those stars in your eyes though."

"Those are all because of you, Joe."

They traded languorous kisses and ground against each other, more interested in feeling every inch of skin on skin than the acute pressure of his cock in her pussy or a finger on her clit.

Morgan explored his back, ribs and ass, as much of him as she could reach. She loved him as best she knew how. With everything she had, primarily her heart and soul. Without words, without vigorous motion, without carefully placed touches on pressure points, they idled in bliss.

And still the energy they generated lifted them inexorably toward a pinnacle they reached together.

Instead of an explosion, their synchronized release was a cleansing spring shower. They came in unison. Hope, love and unending happiness stole away the pain they'd unintentionally inflicted on each other over the past year and replaced it with optimism. Along with the certainty that the moment marked a new beginning for them, their family and a love that would never die.

Joe overflowed her pussy with come though only the clench of his ass and the subtle tightening of his jaw gave any hint of his surrender.

They came in silence.

Staring into each other's eyes.

At the beginning of everything important.

CHAPTER FOUR

Kayla spied Morgan fanning herself with the lovely straw hat she'd purchased from a kiosk at the trendy, open-air mall they enjoyed frequenting on nice days. Unusual for the woman who ordinarily basked in the heat of summer, always trying to talk the gang into tanning by Kate and Mike's pool, not that it was a hard sell.

So what if Kayla attended more for the cocktails and girl talk, preferring the contrast of her pale, unwrinkled skin to the bold swirls of colored ink decorating it? That's what SPF 80 was for. They hung out and Morgan toasted herself golden, sans lines. Which fairly often led to the guys coming home from a job site to snarfle dessert before grilling out. Exactly how their wives liked it.

Today Morgan had complained at least fifty times that the glorious temperature seemed oppressive, even after a double helping of fresh berry sorbet, which Kayla was more than happy to indulge in as well.

Protesting the humidity in a whine, Morgan had actually started to annoy Kayla, a nearly impossible task.

Which might explain why Kayla had strutted more quickly than usual down the cobblestone lane. Well, that and the fact that they approached the shop housing the dress she'd been lusting after for weeks. Their pace certainly couldn't account for the fatigue plaguing Morgan, though. Unfortunately, the other woman slowed to a near crawl, then paused in the shade of a tree at exactly the worst possible place for Kayla's self-control. "Can we cross the street at least, Mo? It's on the way to our cars. There's a bench over by the fountain there if you want to re—people watch for a few minutes."

She'd almost said *rest*.

The instinctive denial Kayla expected didn't bubble from Morgan. Odd, since the woman was on the go all day, every day, running her bakery. A stroll through the mall should not have warranted a break. Typical Mondays, when Sweet Treats stayed closed, meant recipe research, epicurean experiments, buying supplies or component prep for the week ahead. Still, Morgan never seemed to lose her focus or her drive.

Kay had been pleasantly surprised when her friend had texted and begged her to play hooky from the resort for a few hours. Everything, including that mid-morning message, had convinced her aliens had abducted the real Morgan and left this lookalike in her place. Heavy circles marred the golden skin beneath her eyes. Crankiness didn't suit her generally lighthearted nature.

The only other time Kayla had seen Morgan so sullen...

She swallowed hard, afraid to ask. It'd been almost three weeks since the night in the honeymoon suite. Shouldn't she know by now? Maybe it hadn't worked. What else could sap Morgan's infinite energy and perky spirit?

"Using me as an excuse to avoid your dream dress?" Morgan raised one eyebrow at a jaunty angle, distracting Kay from her mental investigations.

"Hell yes." Kayla scowled. She'd successfully resisted the seductive design, hand-painted in gold and plum on lapis silk, during the prior two trips she'd made to the shops with various assortments of the crew ladies.

"Just try it on already. Please." Her friend rolled her eyes.

"We both know if I do, it's going home with me." Kay glanced over her shoulder at the temptation in the window, then to Morgan, then back at the dress.

"Maybe you'll be extra picky, as usual, and delude yourself into believing it's unflattering or some crap. Though I bet you the Boston cream pie in my case right now it would look fabulous. Worthy of the annual award ceremony for the Independent Business Alliance. You know, 'cause I've heard rumors you're about to be nominated for owner of the Best New Venture of the year."

"What?" Kayla's jaw hung open. "Are you freaking kidding me?"

Morgan would know. She'd chaired the committee in her ridiculously sparse free time after scoring the honor the prior year. Her sincere smile wiped some of the fatigue from her eyes. "I can't tell you anything officially, but...congratulations. You'd be better off snagging that now than hunting for something in a few weeks. It'll be gorgeous with your tattoos."

Kayla took two steps toward the shop door before hesitating.

"Go on." Morgan shooed her. "Maybe it's not as expensive as it looks."

They both laughed at that one.

"Okay, okay." Morgan sighed. "How about this... I'm sure it's worth every penny."

It would be a splurge and a half considering the reputation of the boutique, which featured the latest summer fashions in the ornate window display. Still, she couldn't help herself. "I'm telling Dave this is all your fault."

"He's going to thank me when he sees you wearing that masterpiece." Morgan lagged behind as Kayla dashed up the handful of stairs leading into the store.

Miracles did happen. They had her very un-Devon-petite size right there on the front of the rack. Kayla slipped her head through the trapezoid formed by a wooden hanger as well as the straps and bodice of the stunning handkerchief dress she'd drooled over from afar. Up close, it stole her breath.

She giggled as she spun around in search of a changing room, loving the flare of the airy material. Brilliant colors flashed in several mirrors, which hung on the backs of open doors nearby, causing a kaleidoscope effect.

In one of the frames, Kayla glimpsed Morgan sinking to her knees.

"Mo!" She rushed to her friend's side. "Are you all right? What's going on?"

From a foot away, she detected the shaking of Morgan's hands and the unnatural sheen of sweat on her greenish-gray skin.

Clamminess greeted her fingers when she laid them on her friend's brow.

Eyelids scrunched shut, Morgan leaned on the shoulder Kayla lent her. "Sorry. Crap. I thought my dizziness was fading away."

"You're not well." Kayla conducted a mental inventory of the homeopathic remedies lining the shelves in the apothecary at her resort. "How long have you felt like trash? Why didn't you tell me?"

"I'm scared," she whimpered.

The plaintive wisp of audible agony broke Kayla's heart. "It's going to be fine. I'll take you to the doctor. Right now, if you're good to stand up."

"Can I help you?" the salesperson hovering over them asked from more than ritual this time. "Should I call security? There's a nurse's station in the main building."

"No, no." Morgan rose to wobbly legs. She clutched Kayla's arm hard enough to leave bruises. "I'm fine, really. Just...a spell."

The shopkeeper ignored the protest, flicking her concerned glance to Kayla for a ruling.

"Mo... Have you missed your period yet?" The time for pussyfooting around had passed. "Are you..."

"She's pregnant! Of course." The helpful woman perked up, her face illuminating as she clasped her hands over her heart. "Oh, dear, don't worry. This is perfectly normal. Is this your first?"

"Well, I'm not sure yet." Moisture gathered at the corners of her eyes. "I...I hope."

"Honey, I have five brats of my own." The loving tone belied her disparagement of the kids. "The glow in your cheeks is like a neon sign flashing *Preggers! Preggers!* I should have spotted it right off. Here, breathe deep. The heat isn't going to be your friend for a while. Make sure you're eating regularly too."

Kayla stripped the dress from where it'd nearly strangled her in her mad dash. She sighed as she pivoted, intending to replace the garment. There were more important things than the most beautiful outfit in the world.

"Wait." Morgan looked as if she'd fight the kind woman dishing out conventional wisdom like turkey at Thanksgiving. "We'll take the dress."

"I didn't even try it on."

The shopkeeper exchanged a conspiratorial eye roll with Morgan. "It might as well have been made for you."

"Please." Morgan didn't often beg. "It's the very least I can do after ruining your day off. You take even less of them then I do."

"You didn't—"

"I did."

Kayla was stunned into silence. Right there in the middle of the boutique, Morgan—practical, fierce, independent, tough, Morgan—burst into tears. "I'm sorry. Was a bitch all day. You should have slapped me. But instead you bought me ice cream. Twice."

A hiccup interrupted the mangled admission.

"Now that's a friend." The shopkeeper plucked the dress from Kayla. She floated behind the furniture-quality display case supporting a gilded, old-fashioned cash register as if hysterical women had epic meltdowns in the middle of her sophisticated showroom all the time. "This one is on me. You two are the highlight of my Monday. When you wear it, just make sure people know where you found it. Better than a billboard, I swear. Women everywhere will want to emulate your style."

Before Kayla could protest, the woman had swaddled the dress in impressive tissue paper origami and tucked it into an artsy box. She wrapped the package in a bow of some organic material then pressed it into Kayla's hands.

"Wow. I don't know what to say." Her brows climbed.

"Th-thank you." Morgan sniffled.

"You're very welcome, dear." The woman joined them once more, this time extending a wire and bead box concealing mundane Kleenexes. "Go ahead, blow your nose. Take a few spares. The weepy phase can snap back on you."

Morgan accepted her advice with an exceptionally unladylike noise that reminded Kayla of something she'd heard during a show Dave had watched about rhinoceroses on National Geographic. Probably best to keep that thought private.

"Best of luck." The owner ushered them to the door. "Mind the stairs. And come back soon. I'd like to know if you're having a boy or a girl. I'm guessing boy. They always wreaked havoc on my system. What else is new?"

Kayla wrapped her arm around Morgan's waist and took the stairs slowly, in lock-step with her friend. When she looked up, she caught the shopkeeper waving to them and smiled.

"See, there are benefits to having a hormonal, decrepit, freakazoid pal, huh?" Morgan rested her head on Kayla's shoulder as they wound their way to the parking lot. They stopped at the bench Kayla had indicated earlier and two others along their route so Morgan could catch her breath.

"Mo, you're not driving like this." Kay broke the silence that had stretched between them. She couldn't forget her friend's earlier admission... *I'm scared.*

"Okay."

"And when we get to your place, you're going to take a pregnancy test." She squeezed the other woman's hand. "I'll stay with you. Or we can wait for Joe if you'd rather him be there. I know you're afraid of bad news, but you have to be sure. There are things your baby needs from you—"

"*If* there's a baby," Morgan whispered.

"Yes, if..." Kayla wouldn't hurt her friend unintentionally if things didn't turn out like she was almost positive they would. She honestly couldn't believe Joe hadn't made his wife take the test already. True, they'd both been damaged by the disappointments of the past year. Neither was eager to hurt themselves, or the other, again. Still, the insanity had to end.

"I think all the tests I have are expired by now." Morgan sighed as Kayla handed her into the passenger side of her hybrid sedan. "I'd rather not detour on the way home. Not feeling so great. Need to lie down. Somewhere quiet, dark, cool. Please, Kay. Can we hurry? Maybe one of the guys could make a run?"

"No problem. They're going to have to pick up your car anyway. Let me give them a call. I'll have them stop then meet us at your apartment, okay? You can take a little nap while we wait."

"Good idea." Morgan's eyes were already closed, her head tipped back against the rest.

Kayla shut the door, then whipped her phone out of her purse. She monitored Morgan through the glass. Speed dial had her connected to her husband in less than a second.

"Hey, sexy."

"Dave."

"Ah shit. It's not *that* kind of call, huh?" He laughed. When she didn't, he caught on. "What's wrong?"

"It's Morgan." She tried to explain quickly so he didn't panic. "She's all right. But we went to the mall, and she's acting... Well, like Kate did at first, I guess. Crazy emotions. Tired. Sick. Cranky. Just off. I'm taking her home."

"Joe! You'd better come down here." Dave's shout was muffled, as though he held the heel of his hand over the mouthpiece.

They arranged for the guys to swing by to collect Morgan's car and the supplies. Kayla pressed her hand to the butterflies in her stomach. If she felt this unsteady, Morgan must be a mess. She said goodbye and wrapped their call quickly, jogging to the driver's side and slipping in. Only then did she realize she hadn't told Dave she loved him like she usually did when they spoke. There'd be plenty of time tonight to make sure he realized how much she appreciated his reliability. No matter what, he always made her feel safe.

"Okay, everything's set. A half hour or so, and all will be just fine. You'll see." Kayla rambled the rest of the way home though Morgan never once responded. Dozing or not, she seemed to relax at the news of her husband's impending arrival.

Kayla could definitely relate.

***

Joe dodged the headlock Dave attempted to put him in. Noogies wouldn't relieve the knots in his guts.

"Looks like you're going to be a dad, buddy. Your wild days are done."

"Huh. Not if I have anything to say about that." Mike saved Joe from Dave and Neil, who danced around him, whooping, tossing light punches and hollering. "Guys. Tone it down until we know something for sure."

"Thanks." Joe bit the inside of his cheek and nodded. He couldn't stand it if they all had to go through the disappointment he'd endured for close to a year. Too many false alarms had him on edge. Could this be the time? Terrified to hope, he couldn't squash the spark of optimism catching fire inside him.

"You got it." Mike slapped him on the shoulder. "You and Dave head out. We'll be right behind you as soon as we stash the supplies inside. Don't need any of this lumber walking off before we get back tomorrow morning."

Sounding like a broken record but not caring, Joe said, "Thanks," again.

His lips were numb and his fingers beat an irregular rhythm on his ripped jeans as he loped to Dave's truck. His wingman never strayed from his side. The rest of the crew cheered them on, shouting good luck in their wake.

Joe reached Dave's monster black pickup first. He didn't ask before opening the driver's side door. Without something to do he'd go crazy by the time they reached their wives. The pair piled into the cab. Dave tossed the keys across the bench seat. Joe snagged them in one hand, jammed them in the ignition and backed out of the new paver driveway they'd laid last week fast enough to chirp the tires. "Whoa there buddy, no sense in wrecking now. Things are finally going your way, remember?"

The click of Dave's seatbelt echoed in the space between them.

Joe nodded, taking a shaky breath. He fastened his own harness, then moderated his speed to something he wouldn't go to jail for if a cop spotted him.

"It's gonna work out, Joe." Dave slapped Joe's thigh hard enough to leave a bold handprint beneath the denim. "This time next year, you're gonna be exhausted, broke and wrapped around your kid's eensy-weensy finger. I have a feeling."

The big man had pulled his psychic shit one too many times for his friends to dismiss his intuition easily. Somehow that only accelerated the pounding of Joe's heart. What if... "Dave?"

"Yeah, man."

"Am I ready?"

Raucous laughter ricocheted around the truck. "Kind of late to wonder that isn't it?"

Joe couldn't answer past the tightness of his lips.

"Shit, shit. Sorry." Dave rubbed his flat belly. "Right. You're not joking. This is like me freaking out at my wedding, remember?"

"No. I mean, yes. I remember. But they're nothing alike." Joe took his eyes from the road long enough to laser a stare at Dave. "That was ridiculous bullshit. Standing there at the edge of the resort, waiting for Kayla, you lost your mind. Babbled like a crazy man. Not good enough, not rich enough, not hung enough. Whatever. That last one killed me, by the way. How much bigger could one cock get?"

"Exactly." Dave shifted his muddy boots on the thick rubber mat. "Not my finest moment. Don't pull that shit on me now. You're going to be a kickass father. And if you're really lucky, you'll have a son so you can rub it in Mike's face."

Joe couldn't help but laugh. As usual, his friends knew exactly the right thing to do to shake things into perspective. He flipped on the turn signal, taking the exit to the artsy-fartsy mall the girls preferred over the department stores he'd have frequented. In, out, done—unless he was picking out something special for Morgan.

Maybe he should have gotten her a present just in case. He'd work on a surprise for her after they verified… After it was really real.

But in his heart, he knew Dave was right.

He hoped they had halfway decent flowers at the drugstore.

"Okay, I'll stop somewhere and get the stuff." He slipped from the truck, leaving it running as Dave came around the hood. "I know where they keep the tests in each store in a ten mile radius at this point. I'll run in, and be right behind you. Tell Morgan I love her."

Dave grinned and saluted. "Sure will. I'll probably beat you by an hour or two with you driving that recycled tin can."

Joe shook his head as he bent to move the seat back at least a foot in Morgan's hybrid sedan. She loved the miniature neon green car so much he didn't have the heart to suggest she upgrade to something a little more peppy or spacious. Though she might have to soon. He was finding out from Mike that a baby required a ton of shit they'd never considered.

The rumble of Dave's truck pulling away yanked Joe from his vision of a cute toddler with Morgan's eyes, who smashed a plastic toy hammer against his car seat, and everything else he could reach.

With a smile, he slid behind the wheel, then puttered off to the drugstore.

"You've got to be kidding me." Joe stared at the empty slot on the shelf where the pregnancy tests should have been piled fourteen boxes high.

"Sorry, sir." A zit-faced teen in a smock with a giant store logo printed on it looked up from where he was slashing tape with his box cutter. "There was a recall on the store brand and the others sold out. I heard they have some down at the supermarket on the corner."

"Right. Damn. Okay, thanks." He jammed his hands in his jeans and turned Morgan's keys over and over across his knuckles. This was the third unsuccessful stop he'd made so far. What were the odds of that?

Rather than waste time with the lights and fighting soccer moms in enormous SUVs for spots, he dashed out of the store and down the block. He zoomed around displays, a motorized cart blocking most of the walkway and a pallet of two-liters temporarily parked at the entrance to the feminine hygiene aisle. It was like some bizarre nightmare, trying to swim upstream to a place every man dreads being sentenced to in the first place.

There at the end of the aisle, he spotted the purple and white box of the test brand Morgan preferred. He stood on the bottom shelf, ignoring its ominous creaking, and reached to the back of the top row, snagging the lone survivor.

Score!

He grinned as he sprinted for the check out. Of course, when he got there, it seemed only one lane had anyone working and that cashier had a huge yellow *In Training* ribbon on her apron. The line looked long enough to stretch the whole length of the Great Wall of China. Twice.

Joe worked hard to never in his life be *that* guy. The asshole his dad had been so many times he could recall. It took every ounce of his patience to keep from growling until shoppers scattered and cleared the way.

The lady in front of him turned her head. Blue-gray curls bounced as she not-so-subtly eyed the package in his hand. With the brashness only age could generate, she peered up at him from somewhere near belly button height and shook her finger. "I hope you intend to take care of your girl."

He tried not to grin, but couldn't help it. "I swear, ma'am. My *wife* is the most amazing woman on the planet. I'm lucky to have her."

"Good boy." She patted his arm.

Some punk chose then to squeeze past, so intent on texting on his iPhone or posting a picture of the outrageous line on Facebook, accompanied by some smartass caption, that he bumped into the lady. She stumbled, but Joe kept her upright.

"Watch where you're going, kid." Joe's bass had the boy turning, eyes wide, before he hustled off into the crowd.

"I didn't think there were gentlemen like you left in the world." The granny beamed. "I'd say your wife is pretty lucky herself, son."

"Ma'am." A manager approached them. "I can take you over here so you don't have to stand in line."

"Thank you." She nodded once, then swiped the pregnancy test from Joe more deftly than he would have imagined possible. "My son and I appreciate that."

The wink she tossed in his direction caught him off guard. He laughed, then hurried to keep up with her surprisingly swift pace. In the end, she even refused to let him pay for his item or the single red rose he'd selected from the checkout station.

"Best of luck." Mildred, his new BFF, blew him a kiss when he finished packing her groceries in her trunk.

"Thanks!" He smiled as he trotted back to Mo's car. He glanced at his watch. Holy crap, that had taken about a decade longer than he'd hoped. Thank God for Mildred.

He hopped the guardrail dividing the lots, only to find a three-wheeled, blue-and-white meter-maid-mobile, light flashing, parallel to Morgan's ride. "No, no, no."

"I'm afraid so." The petite woman spiked one hand onto her hip as though to ward off a verbal assault he didn't intend to launch. "This lot is for customers of the Drug Shop only."

"I don't suppose it would do me any good to tell you about how I tried to buy a pregnancy test there except they were all out, so I had to go to the supermarket instead?" He sighed, resigned to his fate. If he had to endure the shitstorm of a lifetime in order to find a rainbow at the end of this day, he'd do it a million times over.

Hell, this would make a good story to tell his kid someday.

"Don't waste your breath." She shook her head. "Want to pay this here and now or through the mail?"

"Does it take longer to pay now or for you to give me some kind of voucher?" He reached for his wallet.

"Normally, I'd say paying now is faster, but our wireless credit card doohickey's been on the fritz." She shrugged. "You can take your chances. Heh. Maybe you already did that. Doesn't look like your luck is so great."

Joe tried not to glare. "Not that it's any of your business… I'm praying this test is positive. Write me the ticket. Quickly. Please."

She snagged a pen from her clipboard and scratched away at the triplicate forms. Joe's teeth gritted with each swipe of her pen. How much info could there be on that damn paper?

He peered over her shoulder. Only halfway finished. Shit!

"Quit breathing down my neck, buddy." It might have been his imagination, but her writing seemed to slow. He shuffled backward, tapping his foot when he reached his new outpost.

In a few seconds, she was scribbling along the line on the bottom, some indecipherable signature worthy of a doctor. "Here you go. Have a nice day."

"I'm trying," he snarled.

"Never any love for the meter maid." She shook her head in chagrin.

Joe paused, half-crumpled into Mo's tiny car. "You're right. I'm sorry. That was shitty of me. Enjoy the rest of your day too."

"Hope your girl has a bun in the oven." She tucked herself into the mini-wagon, outrageously blanketed with flower stickers and pastel stripes, then toodled off down the street. It had to suck having a job no one appreciated. He'd give her that.

Banging his head on the steering wheel, he hauled out his cell and dialed Dave. After the third beep, he gave up. Either the guy was driving on the highway and didn't hear the AC/DC ringer he refused to give up or he was already at the house, taking care of their women.

Probably the later.

I'm coming, Mo. Hang in there. Joe flipped on the radio as he merged into traffic on the side street, debating whether or not to risk the beginnings of rush hour on the freeway or stick to ground roads. He checked the flow of traffic over the railing of the bridge heading out of the main part of the city, toward Sweet Treats and the small yet lush apartment he shared with the love of his life, and maybe their child.

Red lights snaked along the pavement like a bold satin ribbon. He swore and jerked the wheel with a cursory glance in the side mirror, avoiding getting trapped in the jam. Holy hell, that had been close. In his rearview, he caught sight of emergency vehicles. Their sirens ballooned then wailed, distorting as they passed him by.

Joe cursed the delay, but stopped to let another batch of emergency trucks, these heading from the other direction, join the ambulance. Probably some douchebag—on his cell phone, not paying attention—jacking everyone up. They should fine dumbasses like that for imposing on everyone else. How many times had he been snagged in the aftermath of a senseless collision on his way home from a job site?

Joe eased off the shoulder, still shaking his head.

Finally, finally, *finally* he swung onto their cute little street with its adorable row houses. Most of them hosted businesses on the first level. He zipped around to the garage in the back, then took the stairs two at a time with the paper bag crumpled in his fist and Morgan's rose tucked into the front pocket of his work shirt.

Kayla met him in the entryway with a smile and a big hug. He almost crushed his friend's wife. Relief at finally being here, home, spread through him. They could survive anything as long as they stood together. The crew. His family.

"Morgan's napping," she kept her voice low. "It won't hurt to wait another hour or so until she wakes up, will it?"

Joe laughed. After all that. All his rushing. All his stress and the hijinks of his journey. Just to wait some more. If he could lie beside his lover—friend and wife—hold her and hang on to her, nothing else mattered. He'd delay an eternity as long as he had her.

"No. No rush." He rubbed Kayla's shoulders. "Thanks so much for helping her. I can't tell you what it means to know you're watching out for her."

"No different than she would do for me. Any of the crew, you know." She smiled.

"Speaking of, where's Dave hiding?"

"I thought he was with you." Kayla tilted her head, her brows drawing together.

"Nope. He dropped me off at the mall. Long story. Way long. It took forever to get the test and…" Unease tingled at the base of Joe's neck. "Wait, he's really not here yet?"

The delays had cost Joe at least half an hour, maybe more.

"Joe?" Kayla's hands trembled where the clenched his arms.

His cell phone already halfway to his ear, he pasted on his best imitation of calmness. "Probably just stuck in traffic. I heard the highway is snarled."

It seemed as if years passed while he listening to ringing. Once, twice…

Then a man who was definitely not Dave answered. "This is North Side Emergency Crew #157. Are you a direct family member of Mr. David Rosewood?"

The flashing lights.

The backed-up traffic.
The accident on the highway.
It all came together with sick certainty in Joe's heart. He flashed cold as ice. Terrified, he bent in half. The white paper bag holding the pregnancy test fell to the floor, forgotten. Joe braced himself with one hand on his knee while the other clutched his cell.

Kayla screamed in the background.

"Yes." He whispered something close to the truth. "I'm his brother."

"There's been an accident." The no-nonsense voice barked out instructions that resonated through the panic in Joe's soul. He noted the hospital the man indicated, repeating it back as commanded.

"Is Dave okay? What happened?" Joe probed for details.

"I can't give you that information over the phone. Hell, I'm not even supposed to have answered. But I got a family too. Meet your brother over at the hospital. Get there fast as you can. And if you believe in praying, you might want to try that. We're doing everything we can."

Joe still held the disconnected phone, staring at the screen while Kayla alternated biting the knuckles of her fist and pummeling his shoulders. No matter the pain she inflicted, he couldn't seem to unfreeze. Until a tired, weak imitation of Morgan's voice called from their bedroom doorway. He peered over his shoulder at her, scrambling to stretch himself upright.

"What's happening?" She pressed her hands to her stomach. "I thought I heard yelling."

"It's Dave." Joe couldn't believe he got the two syllables past the bile and terror swirling in his throat. "There's been an accident. It's bad."

"Oh, God." Morgan reached out to steady herself on the jamb, but Joe saw her losing the battle with gravity.

He dove toward his wife, cradling her against his chest as she fainted. But the motion left Kayla alone. Without him to block her, she charged out the door. He couldn't be in two places at once. Refusing to fail his friend in this too, he deposited Morgan gently on the sofa, then chased after Kay.

CHAPTER FIVE

Kayla's world instantly leeched of all color, life and happiness. Black and white shapes swirled around her. She could think of nothing but closing the distance between her and her soul mate.

Dave needed her. She should never have ignored the discordant rumblings in her gut when he hadn't answered her call or texts. He never failed to know when she needed him.

Horror the likes of which she'd never experienced before drove her to fly down the stairs. She didn't care that she slipped on one of the risers. The descent went quicker as she slid, twisting her ankle just a bit.

"Whoa, there." Neil absorbed the full impact of her weight and the momentum she'd gathered as she tumbled. He staggered a few steps, but didn't fall. Instead, he blanketed her in the warmth of his sinewy arms. "Where's the fire?"

James and Devon giggled from behind their partner.

The lighthearted tinkle didn't linger when they caught sight of her face. Tears streamed down her cheeks. She wouldn't have known except Devon tucked in beside her mate and reached up, brushing them away with her thumb. "Oh no, Morgan wasn't really pregnant?"

"No," Kayla sobbed.

"Shit." Neil brushed his chin over her head, trying to comfort her. "That blows, but we can try again. It'll be fun."

No amount of thrashing could break Kay free of the prison of his embrace. Too strong for his own good, he didn't realize he trapped her. She wasn't proud, but she bit him. Hard.

"Ouch! Damn." He let go, buffing the ache she'd inflicted. "What—?"

"It's not that." Devon understood. She lunged for Kayla's wrist, wrapping her fingers around it. "Something else is fucked up. Wait. Kay. Let us help you. Tell us how. Anything. Just not on your own."

James approached from the other side, speaking calmly, his hands held palms-out as though she were a wild animal. "We're not stopping you. Just want to go with you. We'll drive. You're too upset. Where are we going?"

"H-hos-pital." She surrendered an undignified screech.

"Oh, no." James encroached on her space. "Dave. His truck isn't here."

"Acc—" Her teeth chattered so hard she couldn't say the rest. She didn't have to.

"Okay, okay. In the car, honey." James ushered her into the backseat while Neil bolted for the apartment to snag the keys. Joe collided with him at the top of the landing. They discussed for two seconds before disappearing into the apartment.

Soft hands angled Kayla's face toward Devon, who snuggled up to her side on the bench seat. "Focus on me for a second. We're going to get through this together. I'm going to ask you some questions, yes or no. Just nod if you can, okay?"

Kay's nod came out more like a jerk.

"Good, good." Devon petted her all over. She might have enjoyed the bold caresses from the usually timid woman any other time. Her system was attuned to the touch. Comfort permeated the shell of ragged emotions hardening around her.

"We're going to the hospital, right?"

Kayla bobbed her head hard enough to fling tears onto her shirt. She didn't worry for one second about what Devon would think of that. The other woman offered unconditional support, and Kayla intended to seize it with both trembling hands.

"Which one, sweetheart?" Devon might have been the smaller of the two, but she still managed to rock Kayla, hugging her tight.

"S-Sa..."

"Shit, sorry. St. Anthony's?" Dev supplied the missing link.

Kayla nodded again. Before she could get frustrated by the delay, the door beside her opened. Joe stood there with a floppy Morgan in his arms.

"Ah, crap." Devon tugged on Kayla's belt loops, dragging her to the center of the backseat. "Looks like we need to make some room. Squeeze in next to me, Kay. We can fit. Not much different than piling into your bed that time after the guys went ice fishing."

All Kayla could remember was the heat and pressure of Dave, riding her from behind, sheltering her after the storm of their passion had rained out. Oh God. What would she do without that? He had to be okay. She would know if he wasn't. Surely if the bright flame of his spirit had extinguished, she would have died along with him, their hearts so entangled that a visceral bond had formed.

She buried her face in Devon's neck and sobbed. Huddled close as could be, they sank when the seat dipped behind her as Joe somehow must have contorted himself into the backseat, still cradling his groggy, though conscious, wife. James and Neil claimed the front.

"St. Anthony's," Devon muttered to one of her men.

Kayla couldn't bother to look up long enough to see which drove them to find out her fate. She guessed it was Neil when James spoke low, yet urgently, into his phone. "Mike. Yeah, not good. No. We don't know about the baby yet. But... It's Dave. There's been an accident. It's serious. No other news. Meet us at St. Anthony's."

Devon reached around to buckle herself in then help Kayla with her seatbelt. Dave was always so conscious of safety. She could only hope today had been no exception. This extended family of hers was her world, but without Dave, there was no universe to exist in.

She hiccupped, struggling to draw in a breath despite the stars dancing behind her lids. Dave needed her, she had to be strong for him.

Don't give up, Dave.
I'll be with you soon, I promise.
I would take your pain if I could.
You're not alone. Never.
I swear I'll do everything I can to help you.
Just don't surrender.
I can't live without you.

Please. Please. Please.

Thoughts rolled through her mind. Rapid, strong and endless, her litany drowned out anything her friends attempted to communicate. All she understood was that they were there. By her side.

Dev squeezed her fingers and Joe did his best to shelter both Morgan and her with the angle of his broad body. James shifted in his seat to lay a palm on her knee. She didn't look up again until the car screeched to a halt under the portico of the emergency ward of the hospital.

Then she practically climbed over Devon to exit first.

James and Dev each grabbed one of her hands. They ran beside her through the automatic doors and skidded to the first nurse's station in sight, relieved to find Mike and Kate playing good cop, bad cop with the harried woman behind the polished glass island.

"Here. See." Mike held out his arms for Kay. "This is his wife."

"And the rest of you are his *brothers*? Short, tall, blond, brunette, skinny and ripped?" She *hurrumphed* as she scanned their features. Neil and Joe straggled in. "What do we have here? A long-lost sister too? What's wrong with that girl?"

Joe held Morgan so the nurse could inspect her. Despite her weak protests, he didn't seem like he planned to set her down any time soon. "My wife fainted. And I think she might be pregnant. Please help?"

"Oh, you kids are just making my day." The thick, older woman shook her head. Her cheeks might have gotten more colorful. The sexy café-au-lait shade of her skin made it more difficult to tell. She shouted over her shoulder. "Mel, we need a bed. Pronto. As soon as we send the rest of this gang to the trauma waiting room."

"Trauma? What does that mean? Somebody please tell me something." Kayla begged for more information. She peeked at the nurse's nametag. "Anything, Ms. Ofelia."

"Your guy is in surgery, honey." Her gruff exterior melted around the edges. "This is where I'm supposed to say I don't know squat and tell you to wait it out, but I'm not going to bullshit you. I chatted up one of the EMTs in the break room. He looked as if he'd spent a day digging a ditch with his bare hands. Exhausted, you know? Sometimes we give everything we have to this place, to our patients, and it's not enough. He had that look. Things are grim. They almost lost your husband a few times in the ambulance on the way here."

Kate cried out. Mike drew her close to his side, chaffing her arms until she nodded, inhaling slow and deep through her nose.

"He bled a ton. If he weren't such a beast of a man, he probably wouldn't have stood a chance at all. They got him patched up as best they could. His left leg is causing the most concern right now. They might not be able to save it. And if they can, it won't be pretty. I'm sorry."

His leg? Kayla couldn't give a shit right then. "But Dave? He..."

"You're going to have to wait and see. Even after all that, they're gonna have to run a battery of tests. No telling what else got banged up that they can't see straight off. We can't issue guarantees here, I'm sorry. It was a horrible accident. They're giving him every chance they can. Now he has to fight."

"He will." Mike spun from Kate to brace Kayla with one hand on each of her shoulders, his elbows locked. "You hear me? He will battle with every breath to stay with you. Do not give up on him. He's stubborn and strong. You'll see."

"Listen to your friend. Errr, brother-in-law." Ofelia scrunched up her nose. "Whatever you want to call him. I've been around long enough to know a person's soul makes all the difference. And if you're part of our patient's, then you fight with him."

"I will. I am." Kayla nodded, straightening her spine. Neil, James, and Devon flanked her.

"Good." The nurse pointed down a long hall glowing with florescent lights. "Third left, follow the signs. The surgeon will come find you as soon as he's finished. Don't get antsy. If things go well, it's gonna take quite a while. Quick news is bad news in this case."

Kayla gulped, then nodded.

The crew led her away.

***

"Not you." Ofelia's arm shot out, stopping Joe. "Bring your girl in here. We'll straighten her out and see if you're going to be a dad. Sound like fun?"

"Yeah." Joe didn't try to hide the tear that plopped onto Morgan's forehead, rousing her a bit more.

"Oh, Joe." She alarmed him when she couldn't seem to say more than that.

"Was that a happy one, or the scared shitless variety?" Ofelia asked him quietly.

"Maybe some of both." He sniffed discretely. "Hoping to grow our family. Not shrink it."

"I'm rooting for you too." The nurse patted his shoulder as they veered off from the rest of the crew. "You kids seem like you deserve to catch a break. But you're a hell of a lot luckier than most I encounter. You've got some crazy thing between you. Not everyone has a support group that tight. You're going to be okay, no matter what happens here today. Trust me."

Joe swallowed hard. "I'm trying."

He set Morgan gently on the gurney, sighing as Ofelia shooed him back a few paces. Morgan's fingers slipped through his, barely clinging when he withdrew. He winced when he watched Ofelia hook Morgan to all kinds of machines and swallowed hard when she inserted the needle with the IV beneath Morgan's delicate skin, though she didn't even flinch.

"Oh, sweet stuff. You're gonna have to toughen up. If she's preggo, you'll see a hell of a lot worse than that in the next nine months." The nurse chuckled. "Nothing we can't fix here, kids. Fatigue, dehydration and likely some wacky hormone crapola. Look at how I can pinch the skin on her hand and it stays. I'm guessing she's been suffering a few bouts of sickness and hasn't wanted to worry your fine ass."

"Is that true?" Joe canted his head.

Morgan didn't deny it. Her lids fluttered closed instead.

Joe didn't bother pursuing the topic. Especially not when she visibly relaxed, her breathing evened out and some of the lines around her eyes vanished.

Another woman entered the room, wheeling a cart of supplies. She was young, pretty, blonde, and something about her niggled Joe's memory. *Please, don't let her be a chick the crew played with.* He honestly couldn't remember some of them. They hadn't been Mo. That's all he knew.

"Oh, Morgan!" The woman rushed to the bed and started flipping through the mostly blank charts, assessing the situation for herself.

"You know this girl?" Ofelia perked up. She snatched a few items off the cart, then worked efficiently doing things Joe couldn't quite see. "Today just gets better and better."

"I went to school with her." She waved smelling salts beneath Morgan's nose, then began to talk low and sweet. "Hey there, Mo. It's Melody Cramer."

Melody. Oh, yeah. Joe had met her at a barbecue once.

"Mel?" Morgan's lashes fluttered as she struggled to stay awake. "Where am I? What are you doing here?"

"Your sexy husband brought you to see me. Seems like you might have passed out on him." She smiled at Morgan. "I thought you told me he was treating you right, huh? Is that any way to repay him?"

"Joe." Morgan reached out.

He clasped her fingers, trying not to disturb the tube protruding from her hand. Ofelia seemed too engrossed in her fiddling on the cart to chide him for interfering. "Right here, baby."

"*Baby*. Accident. Dave." Morgan gasped. Clarity returned to her eyes in a flash. She tried to sit up. The three of them restrained her.

"One thing at a time, girly." Ofelia petted Morgan's hair. She filled in Melody as well as reassuring Morgan. "Your friend is in surgery. There's nothing to know yet. He's strong and he has the rest of his *brothers* to watch out for him. You gotta work on yourself here a bit so you can help and not hinder. Got it?"

Morgan nodded, tears sliding down her cheeks. "Dave."

"You know, I've seen a lot of families in my time here. Not everyone loves their in-laws like you." Ofelia leveled a stare between Joe and Morgan.

Melody saved them from explaining when she presented Morgan with the infamous pee stick. "I assume you know what to do with this?"

"Yeah," Morgan sighed. "We've been trying for a long time."

Joe helped his wife to the restroom. She clutched the pole on her IV bag, and they awkwardly trundled off to take care of business. Once they'd suffered through the ordeal and toddled back to the hospital bed, both of them had grown silent. Afraid to see the giant magic negative on the test they'd become so familiar with.

A minute or two passed while they resettled Morgan, adjusting her and helping her get comfortable once more. "Melody." Morgan cleared her throat. "Can I ask you a favor?"

"Oh Lord." Ofelia slapped her forehead with her hand. "Do I have to leave the room? Why does indulging patients always mean breaking the rules?"

"Maybe you'd better." Joe had a feeling he knew what Morgan was after.

"Shush." Melody flapped her hand at Ofelia. "You're the first in line to buck tradition around here."

"Good." Joe nodded. "Because I think my wife is about to ask you..."

"*If* I'm pregnant—"

"You are." Ofelia whipped the test with a bright, cheery plus sign out for them to see, clasped between her gloved fingers. "Congratulations."

Joe couldn't help himself. He knocked the nurses aside and smothered Mo in hugs and kisses worthy of a homecoming after a decade absence. "I love you, cupcake."

"Love you too." She sniffled.

He laid his hand on her belly. "And mini cupcake."

Melody bawled at their display, and in his peripheral vision, even Ofelia seemed to knuckle away a tear.

"So...since I *am* pregnant." Pride resonated from Morgan's triumphant declaration. "What I wanted to know—"

"Yes?" Melody glanced from Morgan to Joe to Ofelia and back.

"—is when are you able to determine paternity? Can you tell me who the father of the child is?"

Melody opened and closed her mouth. Twice.

Even Ofelia seemed speechless.

They both looked at Joe as if they expected him to render the hospital to rubble, leveling the whole place right down to its foundation.

"It's okay." He laughed ruefully at their shock. "I...sort of... I can't. My brothers. Dave. The one in the accident. It could be him."

"Whoo doggies." Ofelia flopped into one of the chairs near the window. "Are you trying to give me a heart attack?"

"I'm sorry, Morgan." Melody shook her head. "Absolute earliest would be ten weeks in. A few more if you can hold out for a less risky procedure."

"Okay. It doesn't matter to me, you know." Morgan squeezed Joe's hand. "This baby is ours. I just thought..."

"I understand, Mo." Joe kissed her forehead. "Anything to keep him fighting."

The beeping of the machines escalated.

"Oh no, none of that." Ofelia scolded Morgan. "Your blood pressure has to stay nice and steady to keep your little guy happy. You've got more to consider now than you or your husband or even your brother-in-law. Got it?"

Morgan nodded. She peeked up at Joe.

Despite everything, they both wore identical, shit-eating grins.

***

Kayla paced the length of the twenty-seven-and-a-half-tile-wide space. Precaution along with a healthy dose of superstition led her to avoid stepping on the black linoleum sprinkled in a mostly random pattern between the beige monotony of the rest of the flooring.

Would that make a difference in the long run? Probably not, but she would try anything at this point. Maybe she should dodge the cracks too.

She swore at least three days should have passed since they'd arrived, every racing heartbeat seeming to pump in ultra-slow motion. The clock hanging crooked on the wall proclaimed it hadn't even been four hours yet.

It killed her to be so close to Dave and yet so far away. If only she could see him, hold his hand, tell him she was there. Lend him whatever strength she could. Maybe then she wouldn't feel like she'd chugged an entire bottle of bleach. Her stomach churned when she considered how minor that pain would be compared to what Dave likely faced.

A rhythmic squeak interrupted the now familiar soundtrack of the waiting room—the crunch of Styrofoam coffee cups, people tapping their fingers or toes, snores from the elderly man in the corner and the soft murmurs of various crew members fortifying each other. Heads turned in unison toward the new stimulus.

"Hey." Morgan lifted her fingers from the arm of a wheelchair, pushed by Joe. The plastic hospital bracelet around her wrist slid higher on her thin arm. Rosy cheeks and alert eyes unwound one small tendril of anxiety from Kayla's heart.

"Feeling better?" Mike crossed to the chair and crouched so he could evaluate her up close and personal.

"Much." She leaned forward until her forehead rested on his. "Any updates?"

"Nothing." Neil joined them.

"Remember, Ofelia said that's a good sign." Joe laid one of his broad hands on Morgan's shoulder when she slumped. Kayla, James and Devon circled around their friends.

Kate approached to stand right in front of Morgan. She rubbed her own slightly rounded belly, then said softly, "Can you give us something to smile about?"

"It doesn't feel right." Morgan stared at her socked feet on the metal rests of the wheelchair.

Kayla marched over, taking up a post on the opposite side from Mike. She ordered, "Look at me."

A watery gaze lifted. Tears bulged at the corner of Morgan's eyes, threatening to fall.

"If you're pregnant, no one would be happier for you than Dave." Kayla shivered. "He's talked about it almost every night while we were falling asleep. How much he was hoping for you. How much longer we'd have to wait to find out. Please, tell me it's true. Tell me something wonderful is happening today."

James and Devon wrapped Kayla in their protective embraces. Still, everyone alternated staring at Morgan and Joe.

The tears suspended in her eyes fell, tracing silvery tracks down her cheeks. She bit her lip. Then nodded. "It's true. This time. I'm *pregnant*. It's really true."

Joe leaned forward, burying his face in his wife's neck. If the shaking of his wide shoulders was any indication, he joined her in emotional release. His arms folded over her chest as he hugged her from behind. The guys took turns slugging him in the shoulder, slapping his back and ruffling his hair before nudging Mike out of the way to kiss Morgan's cheek.

They finally cleared away. Even Joe stood upright, giving Kayla room to approach. She leaned in and hugged her friend. "Congratulations. You're going to be a great mom. I'm so thrilled for you."

"And I'm here for you." Morgan clasped her tight enough to border on painful. "Both of you. Dave is tough. We're going to make it through. Him. And all of us too."

"Excuse me. Is Mrs. Rosewood in the room?" A doctor stood in the entryway that had only been empty—and empty and empty some more—for an eternity.

Mike threaded Kayla's arm around his elbow and escorted her to the rumpled man. His scrubs were askew, hair sticking up on end, and his face seemed pale in the harsh lights. Dark stains smattered his clothing.

After the interminable torture of not knowing, the truth suddenly frightened Kayla. She stutter-stepped. The foreman dragged her forward with his momentum. She must have whimpered.

"Come on, Kay." He squeezed her arm. "We have to find out. Hearing the truth isn't going to change anything. It is what it is. We're going to cope with it together."

"This is Kayla Rosewood." Mike presented her to the doctor. "I'm Dave's brother. We're all his brothers."

The rest of the crew huddled close behind them. Morgan and Joe tucked in the rear.

"Big family." The doctor nodded slowly. "I'm not surprised he has so much support. Ma'am, your husband is stubborn as hell. I don't think I've ever seen someone quite so determined not to give up. There were a couple very close calls. Both according to the rescue workers and from what I saw myself. I'm thrilled to be standing in front of you right now and to be able to say your husband is being moved to the ICU for recovery."

"So he's going to be fine?" She struggled to translate each phrase that drifted from the doctor's lips and decipher the repercussions his pronouncement had on her and Dave's lives. Her heart soared with hope and relief.

"I wouldn't say it like that." The surgeon sobered. He ground his hands over his face. "I assume the police haven't been in yet, since he wasn't conscious to answer questions."

Kayla shook her head no.

"Then you don't know anything about the accident?" The surgeon sighed.

Several shallow, quick breaths threatened to choke Kayla.

"You're scaring her." Mike rubbed circles on her back.

"I looked it up on the local news." James spoke up from the rear. A green cast infused his typically bronzed skin.

"You did?" She whipped her head around to stare at him. "Why didn't you show me?"

He didn't answer.

"It's that bad?" She looked between Mike and the doctor.

"All I know is he took on a semi and lost." The surgeon shook his head. "Or maybe he won. I'll let you be the judge. This I'm sure of. It's going to be a long, hard road from here. Your husband was pinned inside his car. His left leg was shattered. Tibia, fibula, kneecap—you name it. A large chunk of his calf muscle was...missing. I did all I could to save the limb. We'll have to wait until he's awake and healing to see if it worked."

"There's still the possibility—"

"I'm afraid so." He grimaced.

"Okay, okay." Kay had spent the last several hours preparing herself for this, based on the tips Ofelia had given them. "It's horrible. Terrifying. Going to be so difficult for him to not be active—"

She didn't realize she'd cut off until Mike hugged her tight and someone petted her hair from behind. She cleared her throat. "But other than his leg. He's okay, right?"

"I'm not trying to be evasive, Mrs. Rosewood. I'm sorry. The reality is we just can't be sure yet. They'll run more tests in the morning. A lot of him is too swollen for accurate imaging right now, but we think we've addressed the bleeding and isolated all the critical issues. He's banged up pretty much everywhere. A piece of the door gashed his belly. He had stitches in his face, arms, chest and... Well, there's no part of him we didn't work on except his back."

Her knees buckled.

Strong arms surrounded her, keeping her afloat through the storm of fear and pain.

"I know it may not seem like it. Not today and not six months from now, but your husband is lucky. So very fortunate to still be with us, given the situation. A few inches more of that door bending or a couple inches higher on the crushing pressure that mangled his leg or... any number of *almosts*, and we would not have been able to help him."

"Dave." Kayla cried his name over and over.

"Can we see him?" Mike asked for her.

"Once they have him in the ICU, we'll let Mrs. Rosewood in for five minutes. You—only you—can go with her. After that, you might as well go home and get some rest. You won't be able to see him again until tomorrow after his exams, and he's going to need you when he wakes up. He's stayed strong for you all, now you're going to have to carry him."

"That won't be a problem." Neil crossed his arms over his chest as if storing up his energy. "We're a crew. We stick together. That's what we're here for."

"I sort of got that sense." The surgeon smiled wanly. "You all hang tight a little while longer and a nurse will come for you. I'm heading home now. Days like today make me wish I had more time to spend with my family."

Kayla's hand shot out, latching on to the doctor. "Thank you."

"You're very welcome." He nodded.

***

Joe watched Mike and Kayla march down the hall behind the nurse who'd come to collect them and lead them to Dave. They trundled off as if headed to the gallows, bracing themselves for whatever they might find at the other end of the journey. He wished he could get just a glimpse of his crewmate. As if that tiny contact might help one of his best friends rest more peacefully.

Tomorrow.

His pocket vibrated. He jumped. Almost anyone who would bother calling him was already in this room. After considering ignoring it, he figured what the hell? It wasn't like the tension was doing him any good without distractions. He slipped the device from his jeans and winced at the contact picture of his cousin Eli, who wore a smug grin while he held up a monster, twenty-two-inch rainbow trout he'd caught on their last ice-fishing trip.

Eli and his gang of adopted brothers plus one sister had grown close to Dave over the years, despite sporadic contact. How would Joe tell them what had happened?

"Hey." He choked out a greeting, hoping the rest came easier.

"You weren't even gonna call me with the news, dirtbag?" Laughter, not heat, infused the accusation with lightheartedness Joe couldn't comprehend.

"How'd you hear about Dave?" He plopped onto one of the molded plastic bucket seats that made him feel like a giant in a kindergarten class. With his back turned to the rest of the crew, Joe pitched his question low to avoid upsetting them any more than they already were. He dropped his head into one hand, his elbow propped on his knee, and scrubbed his fingers through his hair. "Is the footage so bad it hit the regional news? We don't know much other than that he tangoed with a semi."

"What?" Eli's tone morphed from cajoling to serious in no time flat. The hot-rodder might have mastered his cool facade, but Joe didn't have to be told Eli led his gang of mechanics with the same natural instinct Mike used to glue their crew together. The rest of Eli's shop was comprised of a motley assortment of kids from rocky pasts. His dad had rescued each of them after getting involved in his wife's community outreach program following her untimely death. They'd stuck together ever since. A blend of family, yet not. It was scary how much they reminded Joe of the crew when he got to hang out with them, which wasn't as often as he'd like, being a couple states away and all. "I was talking about Neil's fucking Facebook post that claimed he was gonna be an honorary uncle again. And James's comment that Morgan was going to kick his ass for spilling the beans. Assumed that had to be all you. Congratulations, daddy-o."

Joe glanced over his shoulder to where the youngest guy in the crew fiddled with his smartphone. Devon curled under one of his arms, reading off the screen too. Joe had assumed they were playing some brainiac word game together, as usual, to pass the time and keep themselves from going insane with worry.

"Ah, right. Yes. Dad-to-be. That's me." How could one man be so damn happy and so torn up at the same time?

He glanced over to where Morgan had dozed off on a bench, her head resting on Neil's thigh. The tall blond man stroked her hair idly, calming himself along with Joe's wife. Purple smudges still stained the skin beneath her eyes, and she huddled beneath two flannel shirts the guys had sacrificed for her. He felt as though he wanted to laugh until he cried. Again.

"Dude?"

"Ah, thank you. I can hardly believe it's finally real."

"So, not to cut the celebration short, but what the fuck did you mean about Dave?"

Rocketing to his feet, Joe stormed around the corner, frustration bubbling to the surface. "It's bad. We're in the mother fucking hospital trauma center. The waiting room. We've been here for fucking ever. Like, six hours at least. We don't know jack shit. Except that we're all about to fucking go nuts. Long story short, Dave and I left work about the same time. I had to stop and pick up the pregnancy test. It took *way* longer than I thought. When I got home, he hadn't made it yet."

A horrible noise, maybe something like a sob, tangled in his throat.

"Calm down. Deep breaths, man." Eli waited him out until he got his shit together.

"He never made it."

"Holy shit." Eli sounded like he might be running. Breath huffed from him. A heavy metallic crash could have come from the thick fire door, which separated the auto body restoration offices from the garage, slamming into the cinderblock wall.

A chorus of cheers burst through the receiver.

"Woot woot!"

"Congrats, man."

"Way to knock her up!"

Eli tried to shush them. They clearly didn't understand.

"It's not true?" That sounded like Sally, the lone girl Eli's dad had brought into their fold. Tough as nails on the outside, Joe suspected she had a gooey core not so far below the surface, if only she met the right person to crack her shell.

"It is, it is." Eli reassured them. "Alanso, clear my schedule and yours for a couple days. We're heading out there."

"What's wrong, boss?" The guys loved to rile Eli by calling him that. They'd realize things were serious when he didn't bother protesting. No time to waste.

"It's Dave. There's been an accident. Don't know much yet. At the very least we can deal with his truck, get the insurance under control and take the paperwork off their hands. We know that shit inside and out."

"You don't have to—" Joe tried to interrupt. He shouldn't have bothered.

Eli railroaded right over him. "Dude. Let us help. That's what family is for. You're going to have other shit on your plate. Double now. How is Mo, anyway?"

"Up and down." Tension crept along his neck, infusing a dull ache in the base of his skull. "The whole reason we headed home in the first place was 'cause she was acting funny at the mall. Kay called us to give us a head's up. Oh, fuck. I was so pissed off there was an accident, cursing and raving like a road-raging lunatic because it was going to make me five minutes later getting back to Morgan. I detoured. Took the back way. And all that time he was lying there, hurt. If I'd gone the other way, maybe…"

"You'd have been stuck in the miles of traffic behind him. You couldn't have helped. Not even to stand by his side. Quit it, Joe." Eli broke him from the destructive line of reasoning. "There's enough legitimate stuff to freak out about here."

"No kidding. Morgan fucking passed out when she heard the news and spent several hours getting fluids at the hospital before we joined the rest of the crew. I'm worried. The stress isn't good for her or the baby."

"See, see." Eli dropped to a hush. The background clanks and ratchet whirs died down, telling Joe he must have stepped outside. "Too much at once. We've got your back. Look, Joe. I'll never forget the summer after my mom died when you quit your league to come out here. Baseball is everything to a fourteen-year-old, especially one as good as you were. You never blinked twice. For my dad and me. You pumped gas at the station, cooked those horrible meals and did whatever you could to keep me from going crazy. Let me do this for you."

Joe swallowed hard. The times he'd sat shoulder to shoulder with his cousin while silent tears streaked down his cheeks were as vivid as if they'd happened yesterday. He hoped they didn't have to repeat those sessions in reverse. Still, it'd be nice to have that kind of support, one step removed from the pain. "Yeah. Yeah, okay."

"Great." Eli sighed. "We'll be there tomorrow around lunch. I'll call when we're closing in so you can tell us where to meet you."

"Thank you.

"You got it. Call us if...anything changes." Eli didn't have to spell it out.

They both knew what he meant.

"Will do." Joe couldn't manage more than that. He disconnected then slammed his fist into the wall. Bruised knuckles wouldn't help the situation. Still, they gave him something else to focus on. "Son of a bitch."

CHAPTER SIX

"We'll see you first thing tomorrow, okay?" Kate hugged Kayla tight enough that the bulge of her baby belly bumped into Kay noticeably.

"There's not going to be a lot for you to do. You should sleep in as long as you can." She patted Kate's back. "Don't want your little princess getting upset. Same goes for you, Mo."

Joe didn't argue. In the shadows of the hospital parking lot, she thought she detected frown lines around his sexy pout. He tucked his wife close to his chest.

"Okay." Morgan nodded before glancing at James. "As long as somebody promises to text us any updates."

"I'm on that." He tossed her a mock salute.

"Agreed then." Mike and Joe boosted their wives into Mike's extended-cab pickup. Despite everything, Kay smiled softly at the picture they made. Two young families. Everything in front of them potential.

"Sweet dreams." Kate's wish for Kayla escaped before the door shut. The women waved as they pulled away.

"Come on, sweetheart. We were thinking we'd take you to our place since it's closer. Just in case. Unless you'd be more comfortable at your cabin?"

"No. You're right, Neil." She allowed him to entwine their fingers and direct her to Morgan's car. "It's smarter to stay nearby. Plus, I just don't think I could sleep in our bed knowing he's up there..."

Neil broke her line of sight with the ultra-modern glass and chrome building, so unlike their craftsman cottage in the woods. Everything about the cold, concrete structure would repulse Dave. Neil picked her up and carried her across the remaining few steps to the vehicle. Even in the blackest hour of the night, its cheery neon paint glowed. He slid into the backseat and buckled her in before attending to his own restraint. He used his sleeve to wipe rogue tears from her face.

"S-sorry." She couldn't believe she hadn't noticed them herself. "Didn't think I had any of those left."

"You don't worry about that." Neil held her hand. "I'm sure we're all going to be taking turns with the tissues. When someone's down, the rest of us will shoulder the load for a while, okay?"

She nodded, with the pathetic amount of affirmation she could muster in opposition to the millions of inner voices shouting nothing would ever be all right again.

"Good night, Dave," she whispered, craning her neck to keep his window, or one as near as she could guess, in sight as long as possible.

Devon and James occupied the front seats. The four passengers kept quiet the entire drive to her friends' house. No one uttered a peep. Not even when they pulled in the driveway and shut off the engine. It seemed to her they all took a breath in unison, then sat, trying to muster the energy to move. Kayla might have thought she was asleep except her eyes were open and her body was quasi-responsive to her commands, if a bit sluggish and delayed. She reached for the door handle when James took action first, leaving the vehicle.

It was his turn to scoop her into his arms, surprising her as always with his deceptive strength. Though she was far from Devon's petite build, he had zero trouble subduing her token protest and toting her up to their bedroom in no time flat.

While he held her, Devon and Neil stripped out of their work clothes.

"Do you want a shower?" James paused as they neared the bathroom.

"No. Just a warm, soft bed, please." She hurt all over. Tension locked her muscles stiff enough to give the Tin Man a run for his money. Hours of gritting her teeth, endless bouts of crying and the uncomfortable furniture at the hospital hadn't helped either.

"That can be arranged." Neil smiled. Devon ran her fingers along Kayla's shoulders as she and Neil headed for the adjoining space. "We'll be back lickety-split. We were dry-walling earlier, gotta get this dust off before mussing up James's fancy sheets or he'll spank us."

Kayla nodded, though she only listened to half of what they said.

"Damn." James let her legs down gently. "You're done in. Can you stand just a minute? This will go quicker if you do. I know how much you hate clothes. These have to be bugging the shit out of you after all this time."

She wobbled but stayed upright when he released her torso and reached for the hem of her sweater.

"Lift up, honey." He nudged her into the position required to slip her shirt over her head. Before she knew it, he'd knelt at her feet to unbutton her jeans and peel them off too. From there he probably had a great perspective on her bare essentials. She couldn't stand binding herself with underwear in addition to the rest of the garments. Unlike any other day, he didn't comment on her nudity. "There you go. Better?"

"Much." She heaved a huge sigh of relief before scratching at the dent left by the button on her jeans. When she did, something funny twinged in her shoulder. A wince tugged the corners of her mouth further south.

"Sore?" James focused on her with unflinching intensity.

"Hell, yes." She had to lie down or fall. Reaching out with one hand, she searched for the bed behind her.

James put his arm around her waist, then guided her to the lush duvet. "Roll over onto your front. I'm nowhere near as good as you, but I'll try to work out some of the knots."

"Mmph," was all she could muster. He impressed her by running his hands lightly across the surface of her skin, averaging their temperatures and assessing the greatest areas of tension to target. Maybe he had been paying attention when she'd given him lessons. Usually he practiced on Neil or

Devon, which led to a lot of fooling around and not so much serious massage technique acquisition. Or so she'd thought.

The pressure of his fingers increased as he threw a thigh over her torso. Heat and softness assured her that he'd joined her in the clothes-free club for the evening. Kayla closed her eyes and took a deep breath, let it out then drew another.

"That's right." He crooned to her as he alternated caresses with real rubbing on either side of her spine. "You're here with us, safe. We've got your back, Kayla. No matter how long or hard this journey is, we'll be with you both."

The gentle rush of water in the shower cut off. Kay drifted. Sometime after, probably not too long, the bed shifted and more hands joined James's. Damp fingers traced the caricature of Dave she'd added to her back piece as a wedding gift to the man who'd already indelibly marked her soul.

A keening whimper ripped from her throat.

"It's okay," Devon whispered in her ear. "We have you. We love you. Go ahead and cry if you want."

"Don't. Want." But still she couldn't seem to halt the steady stream of agony driving moisture from her eyes and sobs from her lugs.

Six hands roamed her body, petting her, soothing her, untangling her. Someone concentrated on her back and ass while the others paid attention to her arms starting at the top and progressing to her fingers. When they'd turned her mostly to jelly they began again, this time on her legs.

The more her body deflated, the easier the agony tore free of her. It poured out all over the soaking pillowcase like an infection draining from her core. Without them, it would have festered, eating her alive from inside.

Instead, one of her friends focused on her neck and scalp while the others erased the debilitating tautness from her thighs, knees and calves. By the time they'd touched her everywhere, imparting healing, she had cried her heart out and was left wasted.

Gasps faded to hiccups and then to sniffles. Someone wiped her nose and kissed her cheek. They had to be as exhausted as her. She reached out, surrounding a wrist with her grasp. Gauging by how her fingers wrapped around the delicate bones, it could only belong to Devon.

With a tug, she invited her friend and sometimes lover to lie beside her.

The women curled together, Devon wrapping around Kayla as she entwined them completely. James and Neil bracketed them. James snuggled up behind Devon, hugging the joined pair tight to his chest. Neil blanketed Kayla's back. He layered his long arm over all three of the people in his bed, keeping them close. The girls, at the center of their snugglefest, were protected from anything outside their tiny sphere.

"We always promised each other we'd take care of our own if it came to that." Neil kissed her cheek. "This is what Dave wanted for you. We've got you. We love you. You won't do this on your own."

"Thanks." Kayla could hardly get the whisper out. "Love you too."

She accepted Devon's tender, reassuring goodnight kiss as the world faded to black.

Together, they managed to find some solace and rest.

***

The next morning brought more endless waiting, ambiguous test results and a shitload of frustration. Dave remained unconscious. Doctors granted each of the crew members five minutes to make a quick pit stop by his bedside. Neil, James and Devon had gone in first, followed by Kate, Mike and Kayla.

Joe and Morgan waited their turn.

After precisely the prescribed visitation, Mike led Kate and Kayla from Dave's room, one arm around each of the women. Tears streamed down his wife's cheeks.

"He had more color this morning." Kayla sniffled.

"I thought so too." Mike agreed. He rubbed his Kate's shoulder when she sobbed again.

"How could he have looked worse than that? He was so still. So different from his usual self." She slumped against Mike.

"It's okay, sweetheart. They're keeping him sedated so he can't feel anything or aggravate his injuries." Mike glanced from Kate to Joe. "Maybe you'd better hold off. It can't be good for the babies for their moms to be so upset."

"No." Morgan gripped Joe's hand hard enough to be uncomfortable. "I need to see him. To talk to him, just for a minute. I'll be okay. I swear."

"If you're not, I'm hauling you out." Joe didn't give a shit if that pissed her off. Her safety, and their child's, came first.

"Deal." Her throat flexed as she swallowed hard.

Joe braced himself for a horrifying sight. A deep breath expanded his ribcage before he consciously relaxed his muscles. Tension wouldn't help any of them. He laced his fingers tight with Morgan's, then turned the corner into Dave's room. Reality exceeded the worst nightmares his imagination had cooked up. Tubes formed macabre spaghetti that threatened to choke Dave, machines blipped in a symphony of discordant electronic music and wires attached to a sling supported Dave's left thigh in mid-air, transforming him into a ghastly marionette.

Joe had overheard the surgeon tell Kayla something about pre-operative traction for proximal femoral something-or-other fractures. He'd lost track about twenty-seven syllables in. All he'd caught was blah blah blah, multiple surgeries to correct, blah blah blah.

This...this looked bad. He hadn't ever seen something so horrific outside of a movie screen. "Holy shit."

"Oh, Dave." Morgan rushed to his side. The big man nearly overflowed the hospital bed, yet the bruises and bandages covering his face and jaw detracted from the aura of strength and vitality that usually surrounded him. She kissed her fingers, then laid them lightly on his shoulder, which appeared free of obvious damage. "I'm *so* sorry."

"What?" Joe whipped his gaze to his wife when she began muttering apology after apology to his best friend.

"If I hadn't been so afraid of taking that stupid test, none of this would have happened. I should have bucked up and done it a week ago, when I first started to suspect. I ignored the signs. I didn't rest enough. Didn't drink enough either, I guess. If I had just been responsible, you wouldn't have been driving right there, right then. I'm *so* sorry. I'll never forgive myself for doing this to you."

"Mo." Joe closed his eyes and wrapped an arm around his wife from behind, snugging her to his chest. "Don't say shit like that. It's life. Chance. If he'd stayed at the site, maybe he'd have fallen off the roof instead. No one can know what the future holds. Dave wouldn't like to hear you talking such crap."

It might have been his imagination, but Joe thought he saw Dave's eyelid twitch.

"Fine." Morgan didn't sound convinced. Still, they only had a few more minutes. They could argue later. In private. Regardless of Dave's state, Joe believed their tone of voice and any strain they harbored could affect his friend. Dave had always been very sensitive to those sorts of things. Trouble between crewmembers would set him on edge until they'd resolved their differences.

"Tell him the good news, cupcake." Joe nuzzled Morgan's hair. Their joy generated powerful positive energy, sparked by the new life embedded in Morgan's womb. Pride and tenderness swamped him.

His wife leaned in even closer, perching delicately on the edge of the bed. She took Dave's hand and, with infinite gentleness, scooted it the inch or two necessary to close the gap between his fingers and her lower abdomen. "It's true, Dave. I'm pregnant."

Neither of them had managed to say the words without shedding a tear yet. This reiteration was no exception. Morgan pressed Dave's palm to the fullness of her belly. "Thank you for all your sacrifices for me and my family. I love you. I swear I will be here every step of the way. Whatever Joe and I can do for you, we will. I hope you know that. You're strong. And you have the most gorgeous woman on Earth to come home to. Sleep tight, sweet dreams. Naughty ones too."

Joe sniffled when his wife leaned forward to kiss the man he'd considered his best friend for nearly a decade. He hadn't imagined it possible, but his adoration multiplied.

"We'll be in again as soon as they let us," Joe promised Dave. "Until then, we'll take care of Kay. Don't you worry about a thing. We've got her. Just like we always swore we would. You concentrate on healing up. Okay? See you later, masturbator."

The only response was the beep of a timer.

A nurse popped her head in the door. "I'm sorry. Mr. Rosewood needs his rest now. You may rejoin your friends in the waiting room."

Joe nodded. "Please take good care of my brother."

"You got it, sugar." She smiled.

He collected Morgan's hand, granting her a moment to toss a lingering glance over her shoulder before they ambled along the linoleum channel toward the rest of the crew.

"You shouldn't lie to a man just because he's injured." Joe *tsked* at Morgan.

"What'd I say?" She tipped her head to the side. "You don't think he's going to be okay? Eventually, I mean. It's going to be hell. But if we don't have faith in him…"

"Not that, cupcake. You told him Kay was the most gorgeous woman on Earth. Clearly that title belongs to you." Joe tugged on her wrist until she tottered to a halt. He surrounded her in his arms, squeezing tight. "I can't believe you thought this was in any way your fault. You bottled that all up and didn't tell me? I'm disappointed, Mo. I thought we were beyond that stage. Look what happened when we avoided our emotions on the baby junk."

"Sorry." She had the decency to look ashamed. "I didn't really understand myself. The grief overwhelmed me. I just felt this horrible dread in my gut. The instant I saw him, it all unlocked, then came pouring out."

"From now on, you tell me when something's bothering you, and we'll work through it together." He wiggled his brows. "I know a great way to reduce your stress."

"Joe. Morgan." Devon waved to them from the end of the hall. "Could you come here? The police would like to ask you a few questions."

Morgan's arm tensed in his grip. "I know hearing about it won't change anything. It scares me, though. To know. To speculate about just how close we came to losing him. Plus I'm sorry, I do still feel responsible."

"We'll get to that in a minute." Joe kissed her knuckles. "If you'd rather go to the cafeteria, I can come find you when this is finished."

"Being away from you is worse." She laid her head on his shoulder even as they picked up their pace. "Let's get through this, then maybe we can go find some lunch. Even though we slept in late, I'm really wishing I could take a nap right about now."

"Remember what Ofelia said." Joe evaluated the dark rings under Morgan's eyes. "Everything about your body is different. Listen to what it's telling you. We'll take some time out. Catch a rest, okay?"

She bit her lip, then nodded.

When they rounded the corner, they found the rest of the crew, along with Joe's cousin Eli and one of his mechanics, Alanso Diaz, gathered around a young police officer. His explanation was already in process. Even he brushed a hand over his close-shaved hair before he got to the meat of the matter.

Grimacing, he turned toward Kayla. James and Neil flanked her, each man cupping one of her elbows in their dinged up hands. "Eyewitnesses corroborate the report from the skid analysis. The brakes went out on a semi. We're verifying the records now, but his rig hadn't maintained inspections. After what I saw in the field yesterday, I'd be glad to testify as an expert witness for your family. The truck hopped the barrier and came at your husband head-on. The tracks on the road show he attempted to avoid the collision and probably mitigated the impact as much as possible, but the bumper of the eighteen-wheeler caught the bed of his pickup and spun it around. The guys I talked to said they think three or maybe four cars hit him as he veered off the road."

Kayla didn't utter a single word. Her face went ashen.

Alanso cursed violently in Spanish from the rear of the group.

"What about everyone else?" Devon asked in a whisper.

The cop shook his head. "There were five fatalities. I haven't been at this all that long, four years now, but this is the worst I've seen. Hopefully for a long time. The truck jackknifed, then rolled. Driver was killed instantly. The trailer crushed a car being driven by an elderly couple who had no chance. Two of the cars that careened into your friend's truck also didn't fare as well. His skilled driving, the safe following distance the witnesses said he maintained and an epic stroke of good luck helped your friend make the best of a nasty situation. About a half dozen other people are seriously to critically injured, though it looks like all of them will pull through now. I would have been here last night, but it's been a total cluster getting this all sorted out."

Joe had to stop his train of thought when it imagined, all too vividly, those horrifying moments Dave had spent wrestling his truck through the chaos.

"When you have a chance, we'll need you to come down to the lot, take some pictures for insurance and let us know what to do with your husband's vehicle." The officer didn't sound as though there were anything to salvage.

"We can take care of that." Eli nodded when Mike looked to him and Alanso. "No problem."

Morgan trembled beneath Joe's arm. He gazed down at his wife, alarmed to find her unsteady on her feet, hooded eyes half closed. "I think Mo's had enough for now. Mike, you mind if we crash at your place for lunch and a nap since you're closest? We'll come back this afternoon for a shift with Kay."

"Really, you should all take a break." Kayla's monotone hurt Joe's heart. "There's nothing we can do now. They've declared him stable. Go ahead, Mike. Take Kate too. Eli and Alanso can meet you back there to catch up. No reason this should be all doom and gloom. You don't get to see each other often, and I can tell this is draining everyone."

"What about you?" Kate tried to protest.

"We're here. We'll stay." Neil looked to Devon and James for confirmation. The three of them stood united, keeping Kayla strong.

"Thank you," Morgan mumbled. "You're right. I feel like a wimp, not able to be a rock for you. Right now, it's just...too much."

Joe followed as she lurched for the bathroom. He didn't give a fuck about the sign marked *Ladies*. He held his wife as she lost her breakfast, rubbing her back and wiping her face with cool paper towels after the bout had passed.

"Come on, cupcake." He lifted her in his arms. "You're okay now. We're gonna go take a nice nap together."

"So sorry. Love you." She was asleep before they reached the parking lot, Mike and Kate close on their heels. The couple's identical grimaces matched Joe's.

***

Morgan stretched, basking in the late afternoon sun that poured through the oversized windows in Kate and Mike's living room. Sparkles danced across the surface of the pool outside, making the walls glitter. Thank God for the privacy fence the crew had installed pronto after Mike moved in.

Someone had laid out the sprawling feather mattress in the middle of the floor. She'd pit stopped only to use the restroom, brush her teeth and strip down before collapsing onto the soft nest complete with the cozy patchwork quilt Kayla had sewn for their friends' Christmas gifts last year.

Beside her, Joe snuffled, then rolled to his side, enveloping her in the shelter of his embrace. The furnace of his chest alleviated the need for any covers. She kicked them off. Naked felt more and more comfortable to her. The crew had changed her irrevocably.

A smile spread across her face when she reached out blindly behind her. Hard, hot muscle filled her palm.

"Watch what you're grabbing there, girly. The good stuff is down and to the left." Mike's sleep-roughened drawl had her cracking up. She couldn't stop giggling. Especially not when the foreman took advantage of her sprawl to tickle the spot on her hip that set her off every time. The crew hadn't let her off the hook since they'd discovered the sensitive area.

She shrieked. Jerking around, she retaliated by pinching his nipple with just enough twist thrown in that it couldn't be entirely pleasurable.

"What's wrong?" Joe bolted upright. Fight or flight kicked in. He grabbed Morgan, tucked her beneath his arm, and searched for imminent danger.

"Calm down, tiger." Kate half-smiled around a yawn as she reached across the pile from the far side of Mike to pat Joe's calf. A soothing litany poured from her as easily as if she'd rehearsed it a million times. "No one's coming after Morgan. You're safe. We all are. Even Dave is pulling through. There's nothing to be afraid of."

"Dave!" Morgan clutched her hands over her heart, afraid her chest might rip open when a spear of agony pierced it. Breath locked in her lungs.

"Quit it, you two. He's hanging in there." Mike switched from playful to serious in an instant. "That stubborn motherfucker is not going to quit on us. It won't be easy, but I honestly think he's going to be okay. I know it. Deep down. Don't you give up on him, okay? He deserves better from us."

"You're right, he does. So much better." Tears dripped off Morgan's jaw onto her bare breasts. "I'm a horrible damn friend. I didn't remember. I forgot he was hurt. Alone. In that awful room."

"You just woke up, Mo." Joe tipped her face toward him with two fingers beneath her chin. "After being sick and exhausted and scared shitless. Your mind is probably trying to protect you. You should let it."

Kate and Mike huddled closer, coming to kneel beside her. "Dave is never by himself. None of the crew is. We're all there with him. Thinking about him. Loving him. Even if we're not touching."

"I know you ladies probably going to rip my balls off for saying this..." Mike angled away from Kate and Morgan just a bit. Enough to put his impressive family jewels out of clawing distance when he continued, "But these pregnancy hormone jobbies... They're making you temporarily insane. I mean that in the nicest way possible. We won't hold it against you, seeing as how we adore you and all. Holy shit, though. What purpose could this possibly serve in nature? Kate's kind of coming around now. You're in the thick of it, Morgan. Right at the worst possible time. Believe me, this is not the calm, rational woman I know and love. You even said damn. You *never* curse."

"Tell them what you told me at the hospital." Joe dropped his forehead on her quivering shoulder. "I could see you didn't believe me. Get some more opinions."

"What is he talking about?" Kate took Morgan's hand. None of them were fazed by their lack of clothing anymore. They had nothing to hide from each other, she reminded herself.

A confession lodged in Morgan's throat. She had to try to several times to spit it out. "If it weren't for me, Dave never would have gotten hurt in the first place. And now I'm so fucking self-centered, all I thought when I woke up was *thank goodness I feel better.* Dave isn't going to be okay any time soon. He's not going to wake up pain-free for...a *very* long time."

A hiccup interrupted her. Mike, Joe and Kate stared. Mike sputtered but didn't formulate a response quick enough to keep her from unburdening herself. "I put him there, and I didn't even remember. He could be the man who gave us a child. Look how I repay him. Not by caring for his wife—by detracting from her support, by letting some mild discomfort take me out of the loop, by even forgetting *he* needs *me* this time!"

By the end of her tirade, she was shouting like the guy outside the sketchy gas station in the heart of downtown, who ranted that civilization was doomed because people drank too many Slurpees. Waving her hands and foaming at the mouth would be the next stop. As if having an out of body experience, she could see it happening, yet couldn't stop herself from escalating.

"Shh. Cupcake, calm down." Joe tried to avert disaster. It was far too late for sensibility.

"You're not listening to me! I fucking nearly got our friend killed and then FORGOT he was alive and suffering!" Every dog in a three-block radius barked and howled when she really hit her stride.

"Oooo-kay." Mike abandoned logic. "Enough is enough."

The men exchanged a look over her head. Joe nodded.

"Oh, no. Whatever you're doing with that mind-meld bull, you just quit it right now." She wagged her finger at them. "It isn't going to work, misters."

"We'll see about that." Mike pounced. He ensnared her legs, keeping her from thrashing when Joe pressed her backward. Neither of them treated her roughly. Their infinite care couldn't be confused for leniency though.

"Do you know how adorable you are when you're pissed?" Joe's placating murmurs only riled her further.

"This isn't a joke, guys."

"It's hard to take you seriously when you spout such nonsense." Mike shook his head. "If you weren't pregnant, I'd already have you over my knee."

Morgan shivered.

"Yeah, that's right. You like being spanked, don't you?" He pinned her legs with one arm so that he could stroke himself a few times. Then he turned to his wife with a wink. "Do you want in on this or are you still feeling this morning?"

"Go, have fun." Kate patted his cheek. "Help her relax before she shatters."

The foreman kissed his wife. His hands roamed until she winced into his mouth. "Sorry, babe."

She retreated, sitting with her shoulder blades propped on the coffee table, which they'd shoved aside to make room for their bed. "No, it's me that should be sorry. It's just that everything is super-sensitive right now. Morgan, you'd better enjoy this while you can. I think I'm going to watch from over here."

Mike lunged for Morgan, devouring her mouth in a heated kiss. The intensity with which they joined had Morgan forgetting about her desire to break free and continue her rant. Some of the steam bled from her as Joe grounded her in reality. Sensing her surrender, his hands on her wrists loosened, then travelled up her arms. He cupped her breasts, massaging in the lingering moisture from her tears.

She groaned. Kate was right. The light touch already felt a million times more potent than usual. Soon it would be overwhelming.

The sound brought Mike's attention back to her. His eyes shone when he saw what Joe did to her, how she'd splayed her legs and arched her spine at the barest beginnings of contact.

"It's been a little bit now since Kate could enjoy me going down on her." He licked his lips. "Can you handle it, Morgan?"

"Let's find out." She abandoned everything other than the bliss the two men above her bestowed. They knew exactly how to distract her from life's worries. How could she say no?

Mike started at her knee, nibbling a trail up her thigh. Joe held her shoulders at an angle so she could watch. She wanted more. Wanted to give him something in return. She reached for his hard-on with a clumsy grab, close enough Mike caught her intention. He paused his journey to instruct Joe. "Give her your cock. She wants to taste you."

Joe grabbed several pillows. He arranged them beneath her, then shuffled closer to her side on his knees. She angled her head toward him, opening her mouth and stretching her neck until he fed himself to her inch by inch.

The head of his cock felt warm and soft against her tongue. She flicked the muscle over his firm shaft, savoring every curse, sigh and groan that dropped from his lips. When Mike reached the apex of her thighs, she gasped, allowing Joe to advance further into her mouth.

As if he could sense her desperation, Mike didn't screw around. He buried his face in her pussy and ate as though she were his favorite meal. One of his broad fingers followed quickly, burrowing inside her drenched pussy.

"Love watching him play with you." Joe groaned. "Almost as much as I love the way you suck me, cupcake. Having him here means we both get what we want. That's right, just like that."

Morgan hollowed her checks, enjoying the taste of her husband. He was right. Not many women could relish the thrill of pleasuring their men without sacrificing some ecstasy of their own.

The rhythmic flick of Mike's tongue zeroed in on her favorite spot. She aided him by wriggling her hips until his mouth aligned perfectly. He hit the bulls-eye. Her eyes flew open wide.

When they did, she caught sight of something she hadn't expected. Two men stood above their playground, arms crossed, legs spread. She squealed and attempted to dive for the covers. With Mike between her legs and Joe supporting her head, she didn't get very far.

Kate gasped.

The distress was enough to shake the guys from their ministrations. But they didn't panic. Joe laughed when he recognized his cousin and Alanso, peering down at them.

"I'm positive I locked our damn doors," Mike growled at the duo of sexy mechanics. Still, he didn't release Morgan. Joe kept her impaled on his cock. Knowing the men couldn't help but stare, she should have been embarrassed. Instead, she couldn't deny a fresh gush of wetness bathed Mike's still-embedded fingers.

Eli, who looked enough like Joe to really rev Morgan's engine, grinned wickedly. "Minor details, friend. We heard some suspicious sounds and thought maybe you needed a hand."

Alanso might actually have blushed. "Not like, a hand in this. Like, it sounded like maybe Morgan was hurt. Though, I think you all have been holding some info out on us."

Mike looked to Joe. They were his family. Morgan knew the foreman was leaving the call to her husband. Would he be ashamed they'd caught him allowing his wife to fuck around with another man? She couldn't stand to dishonor him.

"Shh, Mo." He didn't have to look at her to feel the difference in her posture. "I love you and I don't give a fuck who knows about the crew. It's not like we're hiding our relationship. But guys, we're kind of in the middle of something here. So if you don't mind…"

Tall, dark-haired and devilishly handsome, Eli turned serious. "Will you share your story with us later? I think we might…benefit from hearing your experiences. Sorry to have interrupted your fun, kids. See you back at the hospital."

When he turned to leave, Alanso lingered, unable to stop his gaze from flicking between Morgan, Kate, Mike and Joe.

"Diaz," Eli barked. "Move it."

"Coming, Cobra," he answered yet didn't budge.

Joe peered down at Morgan. She knew instantly what he was asking. Something about the uncertainty in Alanso's naked gaze had hit her low and hard too. She nodded.

They looked to Mike and Kate together. Both of them added their assent.

"Wait!" Joe halted both men with his command.

Eli spun on his heel. Morgan had never seen the feral gleam lighting his dark eyes before. "What are you saying?"

"Talking could never have the same impact as seeing for yourself. Stay. Watch. Learn."

Morgan adored the inherent control Joe wielded. Mike slapped her husband on the shoulder, transmitting his approval with two hard claps.

"Come here, boys." Kate patted the seat she'd made for herself. Plenty of room remained for the two newcomers to share. "Might as well strip down too. I'd bet a hundred bucks you can't keep your hands off your junk once you see... No sense in getting all messy, huh?"

Alanso glanced between Eli and Mike as though afraid they lured him into a trap.

"I'm not going to kill for you for looking at my naked wife." Mike's laugh boomed through the room. "If I didn't trust you, you wouldn't still be here. Go ahead. Do what she says. Let her coach you through your first time."

"It's been a hell of a long time since I was a virgin." Eli stopped just short of rolling his eyes.

"This is a different league," Joe assured the men.

They didn't waste any more time debating.

Morgan sighed when Eli whipped his fitted black T-shirt over his head. Similarly built to Joe, his muscles rippled while he dispatched his jeans in the next instant. Alanso seemed stuck. His body froze as his stare winged to Eli.

"Don't make me undress you like a child," Eli growled at his mechanic.

If Morgan wasn't mistaken, the man might enjoy such treatment. She whimpered.

"Shh, sweetheart." Mike settled deeper between her legs, returning his focus to her saturated folds. "Commercials are over. Now back to our program…"

Eli snorted.

The contact of Mike's soft laps around her clit had Morgan arching in his hold. She grabbed Joe's ass and tugged him closer so she could devour his erection. If she wasn't mistaken, he'd gone harder knowing the other two guys watched her servicing him.

Lyrical muttering in Spanish had her smiling around Joe. In her peripheral vision, she saw Alanso practically rip his black sleeveless tank from dark tan skin. The colorful tattoos covering his arms continued across most of his torso.

Damn. He was gorgeous.

Kate would make out today. Her friend grinned, then reached up to unbutton Alanso's black cargo pants. He didn't protest when she stripped them down to his ankles along with sexy, bright blue briefs that looked amazing in contrast to his complexion.

"Come on, honey." Kate purred, "Take a seat next to me and get comfy. You too, Eli."

Mike increased the pace of his tongue before withdrawing his finger to trace Morgan's opening. When his hand returned, he inserted two fingers, stretching her with little scissoring motions of the digits.

"Christ." Eli didn't screw around. The instant he settled, his hand wrapped around his shaft. He winced, then looked as though he might spit in his palm.

"Hang on." Kate stopped him. "That's not necessary."

She reached into a drawer in the coffee table and withdrew some lube. Ever a gracious host, she went as far as to drizzle some of the cool gel onto her fingers to heat it. She rubbed her palms together, smearing the slippery substance between her hands. When satisfied, she reached out.

Alanso flinched when she would have grasped his straining cock in her hand. "Is that okay? Will Mike care?"

The foreman lifted his head long enough to reassure their visitors. "She's free to do what feels right in the moment. It's how we roll. Quit worrying. Enjoy."

Kate smiled. "I won't bite unless you ask. Promise."

Eli puffed out a breath. Color stained his cheeks as arousal overran logic. "Give me some of that please, baby."

"My pleasure." Kate went for broke. She reached out with both hands simultaneously, filling each with a steely cock. She giggled when the men jerked, shoving themselves deeper into her hold. "That's nice. I like the way you feel. So hard. You like seeing Morgan laid out like this, don't you?"

"Fuck, yeah." Alanso's hips flexed, straining to get closer to her grip.

"She's pretty when she comes. Of all the crew's women, she's always girly and cute. It's kind of sickening, really. That bitch." Kate laughed.

"You fuckers have been living in paradise all this time and you didn't bother to tell us?" Eli growled. "We're going to talk about this later, Joe. When I can think again. I might have to kick your ass."

"Is that any way to treat my husband's best friend?" Kate paused in her stroking, teasing the men.

"Shut up, Cobra." Alanso panted. "If she stops now, I'll die."

Morgan lost track of their banter when Mike redoubled his efforts. Getting serious, he sucked on her clit. For every increase in pressure, she matched his motion on Joe. Her husband began to shake in her hold.

"Oh, Joe's going to lose it soon. He loves to come in Morgan's mouth." Kate glanced over her shoulder.

Just hearing the effect she had on the man of her dreams was enough to ratchet Morgan's enjoyment through the roof. She shuddered, then clenched on Mike's embedded fingers.

"Morgan's right there, Joe. It's okay. Stop holding back. Take her over the edge with you." Mike helped Joe gauge the timing. They would shatter together.

She switched her stare to her husband. The desperation in his gaze motivated her to let him off the hook. She concentrated on Mike's mouth and the wonderful sensations he imparted. Then she reached up and fondled Joe's balls.

They came together.

Pleasure erupted through her mind. Colors danced like a kaleidoscope in front of her eyes. She moaned, though with her mouth full the shouts were muffled. Her heels drummed on the mattress. Every muscle in her body went taut, shuddered, then melted, utterly relaxed.

Joe took a similar journey. Throughout the storm of her passion, Morgan suckled his cock, draining him dry even as her pussy nearly crushed Mike's fingers.

"You're right, she's so sweet when she surrenders." Alanso's reverent whisper cut through the haze of Morgan's lingering arousal. She felt relaxed for the first time in weeks.

Joe crashed, face down, to the mattress beside her. His body ended up perpendicular to hers. She cradled his head on her chest.

But with Kate out of the game, Morgan felt compelled to help Mike reach the same rapture he'd given her. She reached for him, but he shook his head.

"Not this time, Morgan." His nostrils flared as he focused on Joe instead. "Joe, I need something more. I need to fuck. I want to be in control of life for five damn minutes before we go back to that piece of shit hospital. I won't be rough with our girls. Not now. Will you do this for me?"

Eli grunted. "Does he mean what I think he means?"

"That I bend over for my foreman on occasion?" Joe looked up from his place at

Morgan's side. The slightest hint of vulnerability etched onto his face had her burying her fingers in his hair. "Yeah. He does."

"I'm not going to fucking bash you, dickhead." Eli shook his head.

Alanso whipped his head to Eli. "You're not?"

"Why do you all suddenly think I'm a tool?" He snorted. "Hell, no. If that's what you like... I've just never. You know."

Joe nodded and sighed. He didn't say anything else. Instead, he rose to his knees, spreading them wide while leaving his cheek pressed to Morgan's torso. "Take what you need, Mike. It sounds good to me too, giving up control for a while. To let you worry about everything. I trust you."

Morgan gripped her husband tight. The strain of the past twenty-four hours had affected him more than he let on.

Mike grunted, then looked to Kate. "Toss me the lube, babe."

"My pleasure." She winked at her husband.

He snatched the tube from the air with one hand. Wasting no time, he slathered himself with the gel, then began to prepare Joe. He grunted, nipping Morgan's breast lightly when Mike reached between his cheeks to spread more slickness there.

"Son of a bitch." He hissed. "Remember, I'm not James over here. I haven't done this in a while."

"You can take it." Mike unleashed a powerful side of him they didn't often get to see unrestrained. "Open up. Spread your legs wider, then relax."

Morgan glanced between Mike, her husband and the trio of friends on her other side. The guys synchronized their stroking on their cocks to the pace Mike set, penetrating Joe's tight hole with his finger. Now two fingers—or was it three?—when she looked to the foreman again.

Another Spanish curse had her peeking at the hot-rodders.

Kate was getting devious. She clasped Eli and Alanso's wrists, one in each of her much smaller hands. Then she crossed her arms. No way could she force the powerful men to move if they would rather resist.

Eli and Alanso exchanged a heated glance, then allowed Kate to curl their fingers around each other's erections. Alanso didn't hesitate. He picked up right where he'd left off massaging his own hard-on.

A grunt exploded from Eli's chest. He flushed, then breathed hard as his friend stroked his cock. "Shit. It feels so much different when you do it."

"Do you like it?" Alanso swallowed.

Eli paused.

Morgan could tell Kate was preparing to smack him upside the head if he squashed the fragile experiment blossoming between the pair. At least, if he wasn't into it, he should let Alanso down easy. They shouldn't have worried.

"Should I stop, Cobra?" Alanso looked up at the garage owner.

"Fuck yes," he panted.

Kate glared at Eli when Alanso tried to yank his hand back as if burned. Instead, Eli trapped his friend's palm over his cock.

"Not so fast. I meant, fuck yeah I like it. Don't stop or I might deck you." He laughed at the shock on Alanso's face. Then he did one better and began to jerk off the guy sitting muscular shoulder to muscular shoulder with him.

Morgan shivered at the raw lust on their faces. She could only bring herself to look away when Joe tensed. A moment later, he groaned. The sound morphed into a hiss as Mike pushed him forward on her torso, sinking deep with one unrelenting thrust.

"This isn't going to be a long ride, Joe." Mike grunted. He withdrew slowly, then slammed forward once more. "You'd better hang on tight."

Morgan stroked Joe's face and finger combed his hair, helping him relax while Mike invaded his ass. She didn't miss the sigh he released when he surrendered completely to the foreman. "You're doing great, Joe. Let him have you. Give him what he needs. Take too."

Mike squirted more lube onto his shaft before tossing the bottle aside. He leaned forward, getting leverage on his side to work his cock deeper, harder into Joe's welcoming hole. Joe tensed his arms beside her, keeping Mike's momentum from smashing him into her. The show of his strength, in so many different ways, made her love him just a little more. If that were possible.

Morgan basked in the energy created by the four smoking-hot guys surrounding her. Each of them used another to find his release. Sexual, spiritual or mental—maybe all three. She felt honored to be part of their exchange.

Slick slaps echoed from Alanso and Eli, who had lost their initial hesitance. They pumped each other with the sureness only another man could manage when handling cock. Cords stood out in Eli's neck as he flexed his hips upward. His erection bulged in Alanso's hold.

Mike laughed even as he pummeled Joe. "You're never going to be the same again. Trust me. Don't freak when you go back to that damn garage, Eli. It's going to be like fire in your veins. Trying to stop it is stupid."

"Sounds like experience talking," Eli grunted.

"It's been so long. Almost don't remember." Mike increased the intensity of his strokes. "But yeah. Wasn't always...like this."

Joe didn't bother to try and speak. He hung on and offered himself to Mike, lifting his ass higher to meet the increasing pressure of Mike's fucking.

"Thank you." Mike growled as he blanketed Joe's back. He sheltered his friend even as he drilled his ass. "Needed this. Christ. So bad."

Sweat glistened on the skin of both men. Morgan couldn't have adored them more in that moment. Powerful, graceful and a little brutal. They held nothing back.

At the last possible second, Mike lifted his head and stared directly at Kate.

"I love you." The foreman's wife encouraged him, "Go ahead. Come in his ass. Fill him up."

Morgan couldn't say if it was that little speech or the spectacle before them, maybe the combination, but something proved too much for Alanso. He threw his head back and muttered a stream of broken Spanish and English she couldn't understand. Eli must have, though. He tore his gaze from Mike and Joe to observe as he pumped stream after stream of come from his mechanic.

Mike roared. He jerked several times as he too came. His fingers gripped Joe's hips hard enough to leave bruises, but her husband didn't seem to mind. Only when the last drop of fluid leaked from Alanso's cock did Eli surrender. He glanced between his friend and the two men, panting from where they'd collapsed near Morgan, before shattering.

The force of Eli's orgasm impressed Morgan. After all this time with the crew, that was saying something. How long had he hidden his desires? Only a forbidden fantasy could draw that kind of response.

When he shuddered against the coffee table, his cock spent, Alanso developed a wicked grin. He lifted his messy hand to his mouth and licked a swath through the delicacy there. Had James been there, he'd have come in his pants at the sight.

Eli didn't fare much better. He groaned, then slung one arm over his eyes as his seizing renewed. "Stop, stop. I can't take anymore. Holy shit."

Mike and Joe cracked up. They separated with sighs mingled with grunts.

While Kate and Morgan looked on, Mike crossed to Eli and extended his hand. Eli took it with his clean one and allowed Mike to lever him to his feet. Mike banded one arm around his back and squeezed tight. "You've got this. You'll know what the right thing is for your gang."

"And we're always here if you need to talk." Kate kissed Alanso on the cheek.

"Thank you." He turned away, but Morgan caught the shimmer in his delicious chocolate eyes first.

She hoped they were able to fashion a relationship even half as strong as the one she was so fortunate to be part of. Rejuvenated, she couldn't wait to get back to the hospital and the rest of the crew.

CHAPTER SEVEN

Dave stared up at the thick wooden beams of the cathedral ceiling in the living room of Kayla's cabin. Thinking of it as her home, a place he merely lived, helped him cope with the possibility of leaving sometime soon. Really soon.

He swore he'd memorized every knot and streak of grain in the timbers during the past three months. It was a big upgrade from counting creepy birds in the wallpaper of the antiseptic hospital room he'd occupied for almost seven weeks. Still, he'd spent a hell of a lot of time right here, flat on his worthless back. If he never saw another episode of *Dr. Phil* or *Judge Mathis*, it'd be too soon. On the plus side, he did have a better idea of what constituted a good deal at the grocery store after about a million viewings of *The Price Is Right*.

He rolled his eyes. The cluster of dark spots near the ceiling fan caught his attention.

They'd started reminding him of the profile of his childhood dog, Barker, lately.

"Jesus. I need to get out of here," he grumbled, shifting to his side on the bed, which the guys had *temporarily* lugged down from the loft ages ago. Careful to keep the dead weight of his bad leg on top, he pushed up to half-sitting.

"Hmm?" Kate moaned from her spot, where she'd crashed beside him. He hadn't meant to rouse the ultra-preggers woman. As much as he loved her and Morgan, who snuggled against his other side, he struggled to draw in a breath.

Suffocation seemed like a very real possibility.

"Nothing. Sorry. Gotta get up." He did his best not to jostle either of the exhausted women, who'd elected to stay home and nap with him rather than join their friends in picking blueberries for Morgan to incorporate in upcoming seasonal specials. The untamed section of the property, which contained masses of fruit bushes, was too rough for Dave's wheelchair.

He was coming to hate the contraption. His doctors wouldn't let him switch to crutches until he regained feeling in his limb. Rightly so, they feared he'd put pressure on it or bang into things, causing more damage unintentionally. The specialists hadn't said so yet, but their frowns and dampening reassurances led him to believe he was getting close to being written off.

What if he *never* recovered fully?

It seemed he should face the possibility. This could be the new him. His new life. What the hell use was he to the crew like this? He wanted to run, but he had nowhere to go and a leg that wouldn't support him regardless.

"Need help getting to the bathroom?" Morgan scooted aside, giving him a wide berth.

"No!" He hated how she flinched. Yet he couldn't stop the frustration boiling inside him from erupting in a roar. "I do not want help taking a goddamned piss. You might almost be a mother, but I'm no fucking baby."

She raised a single brow from where she lounged. Kate scrubbed her eyes, blinked a few times, then huddled closer to Morgan as if to protect her.

Bile rose in his throat. He tried to escape faster, nearly capsizing his wheelchair in his haste to climb over the arm and haul his leg into position. A vision of his dumb ass, sprawled helpless—and completely devoid of the last scraps of his pride—across the plank flooring rushed into his brain.

Before it became reality, someone snagged the handles of the chair and returned his prison to level. Dave plopped into place none too gently. Footsteps on the hardwood confirmed the rest of the crew had returned from their outing.

"I admit I missed the beginning of that tirade..." Joe's menacing rumble rose goosebumps on Dave's skin. "But you sure as shit sounded like a child just then, douchebag. Don't you *ever* talk to my wife like that again. Bum leg or not, I'll bury my steel-toed boot up your ass."

"He likes that sometimes." James strutted into view, trying to disperse the tension between the two men. "In fact, maybe that's part of his problem. It's been a while, huh? You've dodged every one of our sessions since the accident. Sex is a great way to blow off some steam, you know?"

Dave's gaze flicked to Kayla. His wife tried to pretend everything was normal, putting away the berries with the same determination she'd harnessed to forge on with their lives the past several months. Even turning her back to set buckets in the refrigerator couldn't disguise the stiffness with which she carried herself.

James had hammered a sore spot, hitting a little too close to home.

"Holy shit." Neil jammed his foot in front of the wheel of Dave's chair when he would have rolled away and locked himself in the bathroom. "Look at your face. You really aren't getting any, are you? Did the accident affect—"

"What? Jesus! No." He sputtered, "I can still get it up."

Mike ushered Kayla from the kitchen. She crumpled onto the end of the bed, with Devon close beside her. Dave was grateful for the bond the two women had formed. He hoped his wife could take solace in that since he'd fucked up their perfect relationship. Maybe it was time to cut her loose so she could find a real man. How long could they go on like this?

"Then why is your wife crying?" Devon bristled on behalf of her friend. "What are you doing? To both of you?"

"Ah, damn. Kay, I'm so sorry." He paused to gather his courage before ripping his heart out of his chest. Losing her would be a hell of a lot worse than losing the use of his leg and that had just about killed him. He'd never survive. But as long as she was happy, able to find someone who deserved her, that's all that mattered.

"You are?" She went very still. When she faced him, a glimmer of hope danced in her eyes. "Does that mean you're ready to quit shutting me out? I miss you, Dave."

"No, it means I'm ready to leave." He shoved Neil at crotch level, forcing the tall man away so he could roll. "You deserve better than taking care of me. All of you do."

Fury contorted Kayla's features beyond recognition. She never got angry, never mind exhibiting this unholy rage. "How dare you!"

If Joe hadn't braced the chair, they both would have summersaulted backward at the force of her impact when she flew from the bed and onto his chair. She wasn't careful of his leg when she straddled him. Fists balled in his shirt, and seams popped as she shook him, rattling his teeth. He could do nothing more than stare, his jaw hanging wide open, when she went ballistic.

And still some part of him registered the feel of his naked wife in his arms.

Mainly the part hardening between them.

Jerking off in the shower every morning and a couple times during the day hadn't brought him a fraction of the satisfaction she had without even trying.

"You swore to love me for better or worse. This is pretty fucking awful, and you're stranding me on my own?" Rage evaporated from her, passing as quickly as a violent summer storm. It morphed into something more insidious and painful. Kayla deflated in his arms. She molded perfectly to his chest, then begged, "Please, don't do this to me. Please don't *choose* to leave me. I cried every night you were unconscious in that hospital because I was afraid death would steal you from me. But this...this is worse. You're a ghost of my husband. A shadow of my best friend. Don't do this. Please."

He gulped, unable to argue against her raw agony.

"I can feel you. Your body responds even if your brain is trying to fuck you all up." She kissed the trails of synchronized tears he hadn't realized he shed. "Stop doing this to yourself. Stop thinking for two damn seconds and listen to your body."

"The mangled one? The broken one? Great idea, babe." He snorted.

"I need you," Kayla whispered. "Don't make me suffer alone."

"I know you're hurting, but enough is enough." Devon looked horrified. "Dave, pay attention."

"You're about to make the biggest mistake of your life." Mike dropped a hand on his shoulder and squeezed. "We won't let you do this. Fix it while you still can."

"Why do you want me?" He couldn't stand the rasp his voice had transformed into. Weakness infiltrated every part of him.

"Because I love you." Kayla kissed him gently. She tasted divine. Like blueberries and sunshine and promises.

"I'm useless." He closed his eyes. "I'm not getting better, Kay. How long are we going to act like things are just fine? I'm not. May never be again."

"Do you think I fell in love with you for your leg?" She bit his earlobe hard enough to sting. "Maybe you hit your head harder than they thought in that crash. If this is how things are, that's fine. I love you, Dave. However you are."

He wished he could believe her. What job would he have? A pity role on the crew? Desk jockey for their company? He'd rather not be involved. Living half alive seemed worse than finding a new place.

"Quit thinking so hard." Morgan laid a hand on his arm despite how he'd treated her.

"The doctors can find nothing wrong with your leg, Dave." Kayla peppered his face with kisses. "Tests are all positive. Maybe one or two more surgeries will get the nerves talking again."

"And maybe they won't." Dave shook his head.

"Okay, so what?" Joe jiggled the wheelchair. "You've already lost enough, without adding your soul mate to that list, haven't you?"

Dave wanted to argue, but Kayla warmed him. Her body heat penetrated the ice he'd packed around his heart. She rubbed against him like a cat, fuzzing his logic and stealing his arguments. What if this was the last time he ever held her?

Something primal in him roared, wanting to make it count.

He opened his eyes and met her stare. Point blank, they assessed each other.

Kayla raised up enough that she stole the soft pressure from his cock, which had tucked against her through his pants like a tracking missile locked on its target.

"Get him naked. Someone. Anyone. Hurry." She surprised him with her desperate plea.

"Don't!" Dave barked at the same time Neil reached for the waistband of Dave's sweats.

The crewmember didn't hesitate. He worked the cotton beneath Dave's ass then off his legs, despite the fact that Dave hadn't allowed himself to roam his own home, part of a naturist resort, nude since the accident.

"Oh, Dave." Devon knelt on the floor beside his chair. Her fingers wandered along the length of his disfigurement.

"Don't touch it." He tried to focus, but Kayla returned, sinking over his bare flesh, spreading her wetness on his aching shaft. They were torturing him, and he didn't know if he wanted to survive. "I'm so weak. Lame."

"When I look at this, I see how strong you were to fight through the pain. What the hell was all that for if you're going to quit now?" James joined his mate in petting the wounded leg. Dave couldn't feel their hands, but he imagined what such tender touches would have done to him.

His cock flexed, brushing Kayla's belly.

She shifted, causing the chair to creak. Joe made sure it didn't tip.

Kate, Morgan and Mike observed with eagle eyes.

"Put him inside me," Kay ordered Neil.

"This isn't smart." Dave couldn't bring himself to say no outright.

"But you want it as much as I do." His wife rested her forehead on his.

"More. God, you have no idea how bad." More squeaking followed in time to his trembling. He gripped the arms of the chair so hard he didn't understand how they didn't buckle. It was the only way he could keep himself from wrapping Kayla in his arms and begging her to keep him, injury and all, even though he knew how selfish that request would be, unfair to the woman he loved beyond measure.

"That's all I need to know." Long, gentle fingers cupped his cheeks and angled his face so he couldn't help but observe the devotion in her eyes a moment before she settled her lips on his.

The unique taste of Kayla nourished him. Starving without her, he'd started to lose touch with sanity. After whetting his appetite with the sweet appetizer, he devoured her offering. Engrossed in their lip lock, he didn't notice when she began to squirm, aligning her pussy with his steely erection.

Neil assisted her in taking Dave inside.

The moan he unleashed came straight from the pit of his belly. He'd abstained for months because he could never turn away from this. Knowing he might need to leave for her own good, he'd refused to bind himself tighter to her warmth. The ecstasy, the rightness and the comfort Kayla bestowed, as if her gifts were ordinary. Fuck that.

"Go slow," Neil instructed Kayla. "I can see how tight you are around him. I can't believe you've waited so long. Both of you."

Mike stepped closer to Kayla's side to see for himself. "I should have realized something was broken. I thought you just were avoiding the group, not your own wife too. Dumb bastard."

Dave barely grunted when Mike smacked him upside the head. He deserved it. Besides, the light impact shoved him closer to his wife. She seated herself on him, taking him completely inside her, surrounding him with her light and love.

"Am I hurting you?" She broke their lip lock to pant out a status check. "There's not a lot of room in here for how I want to ride you. It's been way too long to take this slow."

"Here, let us help." Neil put his hands around Kayla's waist. "Let him go just for a moment."

She whimpered when he lifted her. The plump head of Dave's cock locked in the ring of muscles at her entrance. A wail broke from her chest when he slipped free.

"I promise we'll give him right back." Neil kissed her cheek as he laid her on the bed. Mike and Joe each grabbed one of Dave's arms, ducking under them as they had so many times over the past months. Neil and James each held one of his thighs, careful with his injured leg.

Together, his four best friends lifted him, raising him from the wheelchair and depositing him on the mattress where his immobility didn't seem to matter so much. It's not like he could have moved anyway, what with four women piling on top of him, hugging him, kissing him, petting him everywhere they could reach.

Kayla straddled his hips and guided him home once more. She didn't stop until she'd fused them completely. And this time she had plenty of space to operate. Her hips rocked in a sensual arc that stroked all the most sensitive parts of his cock with the lush tissues of her pussy. Leaning forward, she assaulted his lips while she used him for her own pleasure.

He loved every second of her erotic torment.

Dave couldn't last. Not with the brilliance of her energy blinding him to his worries and fears. He couldn't restrain the desperate rapture creeping up inside him, bringing unwise hope with it. "Guys. Help her. Close. Fuck."

They didn't have to be asked twice. Insinuating themselves between their women, the crew guys focused on Kayla with every bit of intensity their wives applied to blowing his mind. They sucked on the silver rings in her nipples, smacked her ass in the playful way she adored, kissed trails up her spine, and he swore he felt someone's hand nudging his balls as they teased her from behind.

It was too much. For Kayla as well as Dave. She ripped her mouth from his, sitting up to drive him as deep as possible. She bucked a few more times, then stilled. Dave held his breath in the moments before she shattered. And when she clenched on him, wringing him tighter than his own fist had so many times lately, his balls churned. They drew tight to his body the instant before he came, shooting an impossible number of blasts inside his wife. His lover. His mate.

It felt so right, he knew he could never leave her without killing them both.

Harming her was something he vowed never to do again.

"Kayla." He stroked her hair and the long lines of her back. He held her so tight she squeaked.

But when she separated their chests, just enough to peer into his eyes, it wasn't pain he saw there. It was love.

"Are you okay?" She panted the question, still catching her breath.

"Perfect. That was amazing." He relaxed for the first time in months. "Thank you for rescuing me from that black hole. Christ. I can't promise I won't go there again but I'll try my best."

"We'll be here to kick your ass and fuck some sense into you." James patted his chest. "Don't you get your panties in a wad about that."

"Right now, I'm not worrying about anything." And it was true. Since the accident, his mind hadn't once been quiet. Constant babbling terror had coursed through his brain. Telling him he'd never heal, never satisfy his wife, never be the man he'd promised to be.

In the wake of passion, silence reigned supreme.

Welcome quiet.

Calm.

Peace with whatever might come next.

"I love you, Dave." Kayla hugged him tight before pulling off, allowing him to slip from her body. "Please never forget that again."

"I promise." He grunted. "But...is someone crushing my leg? Can you move over, please?"

He couldn't lift his head very far, being the bottom of the pile of crewmembers. Still, it was far enough to catch the glances that winged from person to person.

"No one's touching your leg, Dave. We were all careful not to hurt you."

"Shit. Then why is it burning so bad?" He clawed at the sheets as tingles spread from his toes, up the sole of his foot to his ankle then along his calf. "Holy fuck. It hurts."

He laughed and laughed and laughed—with a generous amount of crying, cursing and gasping mixed in.

"Should I call 911?" Devon got to her hands and knees, poised to scramble for a phone.

"No." He chuckled some more. Relief flooded his veins, making him believe he could dance a jig like Uncle Joe with his golden ticket in *Charlie and the Chocolate Factory,* despite the pain. "Don't you see? It hurts. I can feel it. Finally, I can feel it."

Kayla buried her face in his neck and sobbed.

The rest of the crew stroked him over every exposed portion of his body. Fingers combed his hair, held his hands and rubbed his chest. They comforted him through the initial blaze of returning sensation. When the stabbing tingles began to abate, he puffed out a huge sigh.

"Okay, big guy. Let's get you to your doctor's office. Pronto." Mike put an arm around Dave's shoulders, as though he would lift his hulking carcass from the bed singlehandedly. Even with one withered leg, he still weighed a ton. Physical therapy had seen to that.

"Wait a minute." Dave brushed him off. "I want to try something."

The eight faces ringing him looked at him in unison. Devon tilted her head.

He stared at his toes—afraid to do it, afraid not to.

When they realized what he was about to attempt, they switched their stares to his foot.

"It's okay if nothing happens." Kate stroked his bad knee...and he felt it.

"Don't push yourself." James clasped Dave's good ankle. "This is a big step already."

Dave reached out blindly, finding Kayla's hand and clutching it in his.

"I love you no matter what." She kissed his knuckles. The contact sent a jolt of blissful electricity into his system, lighting up his nerve endings. He twitched.

And the toes on his left foot wiggled.

EPILOGUE

"What the hell was so urgent you couldn't wait for the end of the game?" Dave grumbled to Joe as he navigated the half a flight of porch stairs on his crutches. He was getting damn good on the things and cheating a bit, putting pressure on his bad leg when he thought no one was watching.

Joe didn't blame the guy. He'd be going stir crazy by now too. Six months was a hell of a long time to be benched, doomed to rely on others for most everything. Hopefully, today would help Dave regain even more independence.

"Is that any way to greet your best friend's favorite cousin?" Eli shouted from around the corner of the house, intentionally out of sight.

Dave swung out, then back, as he stopped abruptly. "Holy fuck."

Joe sidestepped in time to avoid knocking him over. The rest of the crew and their women scrambled to join them once they realized their friend had spied his surprise.

"What's going on?" The hesitation in Dave's voice might have been amusing if circumstances had been different. Kayla joined him, laying a hand on his ass from a step behind.

"Seeing as your truck wasn't quite as indestructible as your hard head, we thought maybe you'd like a new set of wheels." Eli sat on a gleaming chrome bumper, muscular arms crossed over his built chest. Apparently working on classic cars was about as much exercise as construction jobs. All of his hot-rodders were lean, mean and not dudes Joe would want to scrap with in a dark alley.

"Well, an old set of wheels, really. She's a 1934 Ford Model A." Alanso winked from his spot beside Eli. He patted the enormous red ribbon tied into a bow on the hood of the retro delivery truck. The glossy black paint job, complete with flames on the front, gleamed along with chrome in the fall sunlight.

"She's gorgeous." Dave crossed the rest of the driveway in three swings. He trailed a finger lovingly along the contour of the oval side mirror. "This is way, way too much. I could never accept this kind of gift."

"Look, Joe isn't the only guy in my family who gets off on surprising people. You wouldn't steal all my fun, now would you? Besides, the gang worked their asses off on this beast. They've been dying hear about your reaction. Don't make me say you rejected their efforts."

Dave didn't respond. His face fell a bit, and he looked kind of pale.

"What's wrong?" Kayla whispered to her husband. "Do you need to sit down for a minute?"

"No. Shit. Sorry." He held his crutch in the juncture of his arm long enough to wipe his face. "It's just that... I'm not really to a place where I can drive. I mean, it's better, but the doctor said it could be months still."

"Dude." Eli shook his head. "No worries. We heard that too. Figured you could use a little freedom. Come here."

Eli stood, crossing to the driver's side door. The motion caused his midnight spikes, accompanied by a smattering of neon blue locks, to bob. Dave joined him, still picking at the foam rests on his crutches.

"We modified more than just the exterior for you. It's got hand controls. No foot action necessary." He slapped Dave on the shoulder, then dangled a key with chrome dice for a keychain in front of their friend. "You're ready to blow this joint."

"I. Uh. Wow." Dave froze for a few seconds. "I don't know how I'll ever repay you for this, but...thank you."

His crutches clattered to the ground as he balanced on his good leg. He smashed Eli in a bear hug that seemed to rattle even the sturdy mechanic. Alanso cracked up and snapped a picture with his smartphone of the two men with the truck in the background alongside Eli's pristine Shelby Cobra. "The gang is going to love this shit. I think his eyes bugged out."

Dave put one hand on the frame above the door, then hopped, pulling himself into the driver's seat of the lowered vehicle. He fiddled with the chrome shifter and admired the extensive detailing Eli and his hot-rodders had crafted in the cabin of the truck. Even from a distance, Joe could tell the vehicle was a masterpiece. Maybe Dave would let him have a turn sometime in the next decade.

Dave shut the door then rolled down the window, wiggling his eyebrows at Kayla. "Want to go for a ride, sexy?"

Alanso turned his head, his eyes looking misty, even as a punch hit Joe's gut. *This* was the Dave he knew and loved. The confident, optimistic man who had been missing since that fateful day, eight months earlier.

Thank God.

Kayla squealed. She bolted for the other side of the truck. With her tattoos and new eyebrow piercing, she looked right at home in the stylish ride. The engine roared as Dave turned his key in the ignition. If Joe knew his cousin, he wouldn't have settled for any reasonable amount of horsepower.

Eli did everything full throttle.

The head mechanic snagged the crutches from the driveway, carefully lowered them into the bed, then leaned in to give Dave a one-minute tutorial on operating the modified controls. "Have fun. Don't do anything I wouldn't do."

Dave grinned. "That leaves a hell of a lot on the table, doesn't it?"

"Damn straight." Eli waved as Dave put it in reverse and carefully navigated the open space, three-pointing it until he could pull forward through the winding drive. He seemed to have no problem with the new driving technique, not that the crew limited themselves to traditional methods in any situation. He honked before rounding the bend and cruised out of sight.

"That was fucking awesome." Mike strode up to Eli and slapped him on the back. "Thank you so much."

"Anytime." Eli and Alanso stood shoulder to shoulder, facing the rest of the crew and their women. "I have a feeling we owe you just as much. For showing us...what you did."

Joe grinned. "So, have you shared your sordid knowledge with the rest of your group? How'd that go?"

"It didn't. Not yet." Alanso cursed in Spanish. "Cobra's too damn cautious. Soon, though. If he doesn't, I will. Things are getting tense at the shop."

Eli glared at Alanso. "We have to be careful. When the time is right..."

"Sometimes, things just happen." Kate crossed the gap. She shifted a bundle swaddled in bright pink blankets to one arm, then hugged Eli. "If this past year has taught us nothing else, it's that time is precious. I know you get that too. We never know how long we have. Don't waste your chances. I was scared at first. I almost waited too long. What if I hadn't taken that leap? Told Mike my fantasy about him and his crew? Where would I be today? Certainly not here, with my family."

Alanso grunted his agreement.

"I hear you. I do." Eli nodded. "I'm working on it. Now let me see this daughter of yours. I hope she gets her looks from you, gorgeous."

Mike growled, "Abby's too damn beautiful for her own good. I'm hoping she'll grow out of it. Maybe we'll get lucky and she'll need braces. And some really thick glasses."

"Payback is a bitch, my friend." Eli cooed for the infant, wiggling his fingers and turning to jelly, pretty much the same as all the rest of the crew inevitably did around the minx. It was pitiful how easily one tiny baby could rule them all.

Especially when she giggled and smiled, like now.

"And you, *mamacita*?" Alanso gathered Morgan to his side carefully. His accent always seemed to thicken when he talked to women. Most of them melted beneath the force of his Latin lover routine. Even Joe's wife wasn't immune. "How are you doing? You're glowing and…huge."

She laughed as she patted his rock-hard abs. "Thanks, I think. Things are great. I'm ready to meet our son though. Any time now. The guys keep teasing he must be Dave's to be so damn big. My back is ready for a break."

"It isn't your back I'd be worried about." Alanso's rich skin couldn't hide his blush.

Eli smacked him upside his sexy bald head. "Will you ever learn to think before you speak?"

The crew laughed. Except Morgan's chuckle sounded strained. She grabbed her middle, then bent in half.

"*Joder*! Lo siento. Didn't mean to upset you. He's right. My mouth has no filter. I'm sure it's stretchy—"

"Alanso. Shut it," Morgan hissed. "Not mad. Having a contraction. Sort of been having them all day. Not like this, though. I think it's time. Now."

Before the startled man could recover, Kayla, Devon and several other crew members swarmed Morgan, helping her to sit on the grass by the driveway. James shook Joe from his daze. "Where are you bags? In the car?"

"Yes. Morgan's been packed for a couple days. We're ready." Somehow it sounded like he was trying to convince himself.

"You'd better be." Eli grinned. "Go ahead. Take her to the hospital. Unless you plan to deliver that baby yourself on the way down the mountain. Al and I will wait for Dave and Kay. We'll come as soon as we can."

"Right. Yeah. Okay." Joe could hardly catch his breath when Morgan shrieked again. Kate tossed him a look that said they should get to the hospital *fast*. It was going to be a long night. Somehow, though, he knew by morning his world would be forever changed. For the better.

Kate handed Abby to Mike, then sank to her knees beside Morgan. She coached her best friend through the now-familiar breathing routine. When Morgan relaxed, Kate looked up. "Carry her to her car. Neil can drive for you. I'll come in the backseat too. Okay?"

"Yes. Thank you." He smiled, unable to believe the day had finally come. He scooped up Morgan and cradled her to his chest. After contorting himself into her tiny backseat, while wishing he'd talked to Eli about finding them something more practical, he reached into the front pocket of his jeans.

"I know they're going to make you take off all your jewelry, but I wanted you to have something to hold. Something to remind you of how far we've come," he murmured to Morgan, love radiating from his heart. Every particle of hope, care and concern was returned to him a million times over in her doe-eyed stare. "So I brought this."

He handed her a pebble. The edges were worn smooth and the stone had turned glossy in spots from him handling it so often.

"What is this?" Her brows arched as she looked back to him.

"Just a rock." He shrugged. "I picked it up from the pumpkin patch on our first date. Kind of kept it as my good luck charm. Maybe if things get rough, you could squeeze it in your fist and remember, I'll always be there for you and our son. You're not alone. We'll do this together."

"All of us," Neil and James added simultaneously from the front seat.

"I love you, Morgan." Joe kissed her, then tucked her head against his shoulder as they pulled out of Dave and Kayla's yard. Close behind them, Mike and Devon followed. He caught Eli and Alanso waving as they passed by.

Lifting his hand to say thank you and goodbye, Joe knew it was really the beginning of so much more.

*If the sexy construction crew were Powertools,
their cousin mechanics are sure to be Hot Rods.
Nothing's sexier than seven men with hot rods.*

After Eli's mother died, his father honored her life's mission as a social worker by taking in several kids from the wrong side of the tracks. Not all of them stuck, but those who did became Eli's quasi family.

Their bonds, forged in fires set by their personal demons, are unbreakable—or so Eli wants to believe. Especially since he and Alanso, his best friend and head mechanic, witnessed the overpowering allure of polyamory while visiting the Powertools crew.

Much as Eli would like to deepen the relationships among his foster brothers and sister in the Hot Rods Restoration Team, he's hesitant to risk everything on a quick romp behind a stack of tires.

But when Eli catches Alanso exploring their mutual fantasy at a known hookup spot in a public park, all bets are off. And Eli must decide if it's time to jump in full throttle—and trust his instincts to guide him through the night. If the pair of mechanics can dodge the potholes in their own relationship, maybe they can race together toward the unconventional arrangement with Mustang Sally they both desire.

Warning: Fasten your seatbelts, this is going to be a wild (and naughty) ride!

EXCERPT FROM KING COBRA, HOT RODS BOOK 1

Eli London stared at the drop of sweat gathering on the shoulder of one of his mechanics, Alanso. He flexed his fingers around the torque wrench he'd retrieved for the man, refusing to let go and trace the path perspiration took over deceptively wiry muscles.

Inked artwork brightened as the bead dampened several tattoos. First a tribal scribble, then a portrait of Al's long-lost mom, and finally the top of an intricate cross that disappeared beneath the bunched fabric clinging around his waist. Torn and oil-stained coveralls hugged a high, tight ass.

All Eli could think of these days was that goddamned ass, which Alanso now shoved out in his direction while the bastard tuned some rich kid's engine. With hardly any effort at all, Eli could smack it. Or bite it. Or fuck it.

Son of a bitch.

Nothing good could come of this obsession. Damn his cousin Joe for putting crazy thoughts in his brain. The guy was a member of a construction crew that liked to work hard and play harder together. Their polyamorous bedroom gymnastics had become obvious when Eli and Alanso had walked in on a scene he couldn't forget. But just because that bastard had been lucky enough to find a whole team of fuck buddies his wife adored—no, loved—didn't mean such a wild arrangement could work for everybody in the world.

Eli had no right to wish for the same. Yet lately, each time he looked at the half dozen guys and girl he considered his grease monkey family, he found himself sporting a hard-on stiff enough to jack up a tank with. Thankfully, the oblivious gang hadn't identified the source of his recent frustration. Though they certainly had borne the brunt of his bad temper, adding guilt to the unslakable arousal stripping his gears, leaving him spinning his wheels.

Stuck and stranded. Alone with his dirty little secret.

Except for Alanso

Why had that mechanic been the one to witness Joe and his crew's alternative loving along with Eli? Probably because they went most everywhere together. Eli shoved the memory of his right-hand man's right hand from his mind. Or at least he tried. The guy had tortured Eli's cock with greedy pumps of his trembling fist while the crew's foreman, Mike, demonstrated just how hot it could be to take on one of his own. By fucking Joe while the mechanics had stared, in awe of the power exchange.

Grunts had spilled from Joe's mouth, which knocked against his wife's breast as he took everything Mike gave him then begged for more. The audible decadence echoed through Eli's mind day in and day out. In perfect harmony with the memory of Alanso's answering cries as he witnessed the undeniable claiming.

Eli knew that if he slammed Alanso against the 426 inch engine block of that 1970 Dodge Challenger R/T coupe, the man would spread and welcome him.

Boss, friend...brother.

And that's where the fantasy turned to battery acid, burning Eli's insides with the bitter taste of responsibility and logic.

How could he want a guy he considered family? How could he violate that trust?

He couldn't afford to lose Alanso.

Not from his business, definitely not from his life.

So he could never seize what he craved. Frustration bubbled over.

"What's taking so long, Diaz?" Eli knocked thick, bunched biceps with the tool he carried.

"We're trying to make a profit here, you know?"

Alanso couldn't seem to wipe his glare away as easily as he rid his brow of the moisture dotting it. He snatched the wrench from Eli and returned to his task without taking the bait. If Eli couldn't fuck, the least the guy could do was give him the courtesy of engaging in a decent fight. His teeth ground together.

"You hear me, huevón? This isn't some charity case. Hot Rods is a business. Don't spend all day on a five-hundred-dollar job." Eli thumped the hood, knowing how the impact would reverberate.

Alanso's shoulders tensed. The clench of muscles along his spine altered the shape of his tattoos. Still, he said nothing about the low blow—or how he'd repaid the Londons a million times over for their hand-up through a solid decade of friendship and loyalty—and continued about his job. One he was damn fine at performing. No one could make an engine purr like Alanso.

"You want half-assed, go hire a motorman from the chain in town." He didn't bother to acknowledge Eli with a look.

Still, as Alanso's boss and best friend, Eli knew that tone well enough. It'd be accompanied by Al's tattooed middle finger sticking up along that wrench, he'd bet.

The defiance made Eli long to grab the other man's chin and force him to gaze up. Maybe then Alanso would see the desperation making Eli more unhinged than Mustang Sally during a particularly bad bout of PMS. God help them all.

He'd never wanted something he couldn't have so badly before. Except maybe to heal his mom during those horrid weeks she'd spent dying.

Terror and a soul-deep pain that never entirely faded turned him into something no better than a cornered animal. Eli lashed out. "Good idea. Maybe they'd spend less time checking me out and do their goddamned work."

A clang surprised him. He didn't quite realize what had happened until a spark flew from the metal tool where it connected with the concrete floor of the garage. Alanso had winged the thing an inch or less from Eli's thankfully steel-toed boot when he spun around.

He wouldn't have missed by accident.

"Para el carajo! Maybe I should've done more than look. You're obviously too hardheaded to man up and come for me. So the deal's off the table. I've wasted too much time on a dude who's in denial. You're right about that." Alanso sneered. "I'm tired of waiting for you to grow some cojones."

"Keep your voice down." Eli checked over his shoulder. Kaige and Carver didn't so much as glance in their direction, but the stillness of their bodies made it clear they caught at least wisps of the conversation. Years of tough living had taught the men to tread lightly in conflict. At least until swinging a punch became necessary. Then it was likely to become a free-for-all.

"Joder! Now you want to shut me up. Come mierda." Alanso scrubbed a hand over his bald head, leaving a streak of oil that tempted Eli to buff it away, maybe with his five o'clock shadow. "Wouldn't want the rest of the Hot Rods hearing about the good life and how we're not living it, right? They might revolt."

"Hey, I've never kept anyone against their will. You all chose to stay here. With me. The door's open." Eli waved toward the enormous rolling metal sheets that protected the garage bays at night or when the weather turned cold. Through them, the pumps of the service station his dad had started were visible.

A flash of something miserable twisted Alanso's usually smiling lips into a grimace. The gesture had Eli thinking of something other than what it would feel like to get a blowjob from the man. That was a first after weeks of studying that mouth.

He reached out, but it was too late. Alanso dodged, taking a step back and then another.

"You know what, Cobra." He grabbed his crotch hard enough to make Eli wince. "You can suck it. Or, then again… No, you can't. That fucking checkered flag has dropped, amigo."

Reflex, instinct, dread—something—inspired Eli to lunge for the man who turned away.

Warm, moist skin met his palm.

"Get your fucking hands off me." When the engine guru pivoted, the unusual chill in his brown eyes froze Eli in his tracks. "You had your chance. You blew it. For us both. I'm out of here."

"You're quitting?" Eli gaped as the bottom fell out of his stomach. "Wait—"

"Hell no. I told you I'm over that bus-stop phase." Alanso sliced his hand through the air between them. His knuckles skimmed Eli's chest. They left a slash of fire across his heart.

"I've got places to go and people to do. There are things I gotta learn about myself. And for the first time since we were fifteen, you're not going to be a part of that with me. Your loss."

"Shit. I-I'm sorry." Eli couldn't find a way to say what for. For violating their friendship, for wanting to destroy what they had or for acting like an ass by postponing the inevitable—he couldn't make up his mind. "Don't go."

They'd drawn a crowd. Even Roman inched closer now. The tough yet quiet guy stared openly at their spectacle. Charged air had somehow tipped off Sally too. She emerged from the painting booth, crossing the bays at an alarming rate. If she got tangled up in this, Eli would never forgive himself. Of all their gang, he knew better than to trample on her emotions. Her heart would rip in two if she had any idea of the rift opening at his feet right now.

Just like his chest was hewn.

"I'm not leaving leaving, Cobra." Alanso lowered his voice. "This is my home. I hope some things haven't changed. Let me know if I'm no longer welcome and I'll pack my shit. But I can't fucking do this anymore. Not for another damn minute. I have to know what it's like. To be honest about who I am and what I want. Before I lose any more respect for either of us."

"Fine then." Eli leaned forward before he could stop himself. The awful sensations sliding through his guts had to stop. Fast. Before the rest of the garage got caught in their crossfire. He shoved Alanso hard enough the man stumbled across the threshold before catching his balance. It felt like forcing a baby bird from the nest. He only hoped Al spread his wings fast enough. "Get the hell out. Do what you gotta do."

Alanso mouthed a plea out of sight of the guys now wiping hands on coveralls and milling near in a semi-circle. "Come with me."

Eli slammed his fist on the big red button on the doorframe beside him. With an ominous rattle, the metal door began to lower between them, severing all communication as completely as if the aluminum were a drawbridge over a monster-filled moat.

The scream of a crotch rocket taking off at an unwise speed ricocheted through their space. Gravel pinged when it slung against the barrier he'd erected.

"What the fuck did you do to him, Cobra?" Sally canted her head as she laid into Eli.

"You've really been acting like a snake lately, ever since Dave's accident. Hissing at anyone who comes near. We get that you're afraid of losing people important to you. The crew's near miss seems to have scared you stupid. I get it, I do."

He closed his eyes, trying to block out the concern she voiced for all the rest of the guys staring at him.

"But keep going like you are and you'll drive him away."

"Stop talking, Salome." He knew better than to tell her to shut up, even if she didn't understand how her insight cut him. Hopefully using her full name would be enough to convey how serious he was. He couldn't dive into the details.

No way could he admit what he and Alanso had seen. What they'd done.

"You better not have let your fear hurt him. Tell me you didn't." Her emerald eyes begged much more softly than her steely tone.

Eli didn't bother to lie.

The hand she let fly didn't catch him by surprise. She loved Alanso. They all did.

Which was why he didn't bother to duck. He deserved the stinging impact of her open palm on his cheek. That and more. Because even as his head whipped to the side, he admired the stretch of her petite frame when she stood on her tiptoes, her raven hair and the glint of her fancy-painted fingernails, one of her pride and joys.

If he'd only wanted Alanso, maybe the two of them could have explored the possibility. But he was going to hell because he lusted after all of the Hot Rods.

The gang held their collective breath, waiting to see how he would react to Sally's uncharacteristic act of violence. Roman stiffened, prepared to spring to her defense.

All the fight leeched out of Eli.

No matter how bad it got, they didn't have to be afraid he'd attack one of their own. Then again, hadn't he done just that?

The damage he'd wrought would be far worse than the impact of a fist.

His shoulders dropped and his head hung. "I'll get him back."

"You'd fucking better." Mustang Sally shook her hand before propping it on her hip and pointing to the door. "Don't come home without him."

The five remaining guys closed rank around their littlest member. They knew she'd hate for Eli to see her tears or her alarm. He didn't waste any time offering comfort she wouldn't welcome. Kaige, Carver, Holden, Roman and Bryce would take good care of her.

They didn't need him.

But Alanso might.

ABOUT THE AUTHOR

Jayne Rylon is a *New York Times* and *USA Today* bestselling author. She received the 2011 RomanticTimes Reviewers' Choice Award for Best Indie Erotic Romance.

Her stories used to begin as daydreams in seemingly endless business meetings, but now she is a full-time author, who employs the skills she learned from her straight-laced corporate existence in the business of writing. She lives in Ohio with two cats and her husband, the infamous Mr. Rylon.

When she can escape her purple office, Jayne loves to travel the world, SCUBA dive, take pictures, avoid speeding tickets in her beloved Sky and—of course—read.